Stepping Stones

Carolyn Ann Aish

Stepping Stones

Beric drew a pistol from inside his jacket, pointing it directly at Michela's head. At this close range, a bullet would kill her.

"Come here, Michela! No one makes a fool of me, not twice!" His voice was hoarse, and with a flick of his finger, he released the safety catch, now turning the pistol to point at the king who took a step closer in concern for Michela.

For one brief millisecond, the king's eyes met with Michela's and it seemed to both that the whole world stood still. It was as though their two hearts were one.

Beric's voice shattered the fusion, "Not a step more, or you're dead!"

What They Are Saying About Stepping Stones

O to have a faith like Sarah's. So often we think that the trials we are going through are unnecessary, but if only we keep our faith like Sarah, we will come out the winner and will be stronger. Stepping Stones has been an encouragement to me in that though others are watching for us to make mistakes, we can keep on.
Thirza Elizabeth Dew

STEPPING STONES is so exciting and wrenching that it can't be put it down. I'm really interested to know what happened to Michela and Sarah's father's castle and the treasures. What became of Elisabet and Alfena? A fantastic story which I enjoyed, now I need the next.
Wendy Shaw

Stepping Stones

Carolyn Ann Aish

A Wings ePress, Inc.

Young Adult Novel

Wings ePress, Inc.

Edited by: Anita York
Copy Edited by: Robbin Major
Senior Editor: Robbin Major
Executive Editor: Lorraine Stephens
Cover Artist: Chrissie Poe

All rights reserved

Wings ePress Books
http://www.wingsepress.com

ISBN 978-1-59088-868-1

:

Published In the United States Of America

Wings ePress Inc.
3000 N. Rock Road
Newton, KS 67114

Dedication

To: Joseph Alexander and Michele Margaret,

Daniel, Keziah, Eden and Jordan

One

The insulting voice bellowed again, causing everyone to pause in their various tasks for a second or two.

"Stand over there out of my way! No, not there; over there where I can see you." Lord Beric waved the back of his hand as the two girls pirouetted away from him. "There! That'll do. Now, stay there, both of you, until I tell you to move!"

Seven-year-old Sarah clung tightly to her older sister Michela's dress as if her life depended upon not letting go. The frightened girl hid her face in the folds of the fabric, feeling comforted by the familiar warmth and protection.

Although nearly nineteen, Michela was just as afraid as Sarah was, but in a different way. She felt she was living one of Sarah's nightmares. Michela had never suffered a nightmare, but from Sarah's descriptions, this was what it would be like. In numbness and confusion, Michela kept thinking, *This can't be happening; this is not happening to us!*

Standing stiffly amidst the disordered activity, Michela—in her black dress—looked like a princess in mourning. Her long golden-brown hair, arranged simply around the back of her head, was perfectly in place as she fixed her blue-green eyes on the distant wall. Michela's pale face was inscrutable; no one would have believed this chaos was her home.

Beric strode to her, rattling a bunch of keys in her face, asking, "Which is the treasury key?"

Without replying, and with trembling fingers, Michela selected the right one.

"It better be!" he said grimly, swaggering across the marble floor, his boots scuffing due to his erratic gait. Almost as wide as he was tall, his shock of brown-gray hair looked like a worn chimney brush. It perched atop a huge kettle-shaped ruddy face bristling with forests of eyebrows, nose-hair, and thick moustache. Shaven pats of round features drooped between his large ears, which again sprouted stiff thick hair from the ear-holes themselves. His wide red bulbous nose and huge protruding belly spoke of one who drank alcohol and ate rich food to excess.

Some minutes later, Michela recognized two coffers—a chest and a box—carried out of the castle to be loaded onto the carts waiting in the courtyard. Guards stood, alert, their weapons at the ready as though expecting an ambush. The coins inside the coffers were tax-monies, collected from the extensive estates surrounding the castle, taxes due to be paid to the king. The chest contained the family jewels, and the box held various articles that had been greatly valued by Michela's father, Lord Raynor.

There was nothing Michela could do. This man, Lord Beric, while claiming to be her guardian, was taking everything of value from their home. And Michela knew she had no right of argument, either with Beric's documents or with the considerable army that had ridden through the gates with Beric at its head.

Sarah turned to watch as valuable tapestries and vases were removed and carried outside.

"Oh, Daddy, Daddy; how could you leave us? Why did you die? You cannot help us... and we need you," the girl moaned. Tears drizzled down Sarah's face, and without thinking, she licked them as they ebbed at the sides of her mouth.

Michela's frayed emotions were beyond lamenting her father's sudden death. Was it just yesterday that Lord Raynor's horsemen had carried him from the forest and taken him in a coffin to the castle chapel where he lay in state? How unprepared she had felt for such bad news. *But how can one ever be prepared for...death?* Michela wondered sadly. How shocked she had been, but no tears had come. She wondered why she had not cried. *I will never cry,* she told herself. *Our father left us in such debt to... that man... Beric. How could Father have done this to us? Why did he not tell me? How could he sign that document, giving Beric rights over Sarah and me and the castle if something unforeseen happened? Father should never have trusted a man like that... but perhaps... perhaps... I did not know my father...*

Sarah gave the cry of a wounded kitten, and Michela saw that the chapel itself was being stripped of its treasures—the golden chalice and tray for communion, velvet covers and embroidered cloths, tapestries and floor-coverings.

"Oh Michela, they're taking everything, and most of it's going to be sold!" the girl cried.

Michela wondered what would become of their home.

"Where will the villagers go to worship?" Sarah asked.

Michela did not answer but chilled with a sudden thought. *There'll be no worship. God has forgotten us.*

Beric strode to them again, his eyes bulging and his stance threatening. He sickened her but she refused to allow him to intimidate her. She had been schooled to look people in the eye.

"Right! Get yourselves outside and into the carriage..." Beric stopped mid-sentence as Sarah ran from Michela's side to a slave who carried the large leather-bound Bible. With her hands on the beloved book, the girl tried to halt his exit. In surprise, he stood still. Laying her head on the large book, Sarah cried, "No, please! Don't take the Bible away; please don't sell our Bible!"

In a few ungainly strides, Beric gripped Sarah by her upper arm, twirling her around to face him. With an open hand, he slapped her full in the face, at the same time releasing her so that she fell like a rag doll across the marble flagstones. The child was still for a second or two. Sarah's small frame convulsed, then her heart-wrenching cry drew Michela's feet into flight toward the sister that Beric had clouted out of the way, like a clod of mud.

Snatching her sister up off of the floor, Michela enveloped her, rocking her as a mother would a wounded baby. Looking around for support and assistance, Michela remembered that all of their employees had been dismissed—forcibly ordered to leave. When Beric and his henchmen had arrived, early that morning, the horsemen and footmen were instructed that if they sought re-employment, they were to go to Beric's castle in Clifton. The workers remaining in Rayburn Castle—inside and outside—were all Beric's: the slaves, the servants, the footmen and the armed guards. Michela drew a ragged breath and held Sarah tightly while realizing, *No one is coming to our rescue, they're carrying on as if this treatment is normal.*

"Get up!" Beric shouted, hovering over the pair, his hands on his huge hips. Michela suddenly felt afraid—the man was drooling in satisfaction from his anger! As she struggled to obey this beast that claimed to be their guardian, he reached over and wrenched Sarah from her, shouting at the hysterical child, "Shut up, or I'll shut you up!" He raised his hand.

Michela lost her control and wrested Sarah back again, thrusting the small girl behind her skirt. Sarah, gulping and sobbing in panic, fell to the floor again.

"You will not strike my sister!" Michela said, her eyes blazing into Beric's.

Without hesitating, Beric's palm smacked across Michela's cheek, and then with the same hand, he backhanded the other cheek. Although she recoiled, first one way, then the other, Michela turned her head back to face him. Raising her chin even higher, she stared at Beric in defiance. In the back of her mind, Michela told herself bitterly that he was not a man; he was a worm, with the intestines of a chicken and the self-control of a mushroom.

"Tell her to stop bawling, or I'll have her whipped! And you too!"

Michela felt stunned, but did not take her eyes off him. She could hear Sarah's faltering, long-drawn sobs. Threats of whipping were foreign to Michela and Sarah. The older girl thought he could not be serious.

Looking toward the door, Beric bellowed, "Get Percival! Tell him to bring his whip!"

Without moving or turning for fear he would strike again, Michela mustered her most commanding tone, and said, "Sarah! Stop crying!"

Feeling she was going to vomit, Sarah had heard and understood the exchange. She clamped her hands over her mouth and managed to muffle her sobs by holding her breath.

Beric turned away, waving his hand at the slaves as if they had stopped working, but they had scarcely paused.

Percival strode into the great hall. He was as tall and thin as Beric was short and fat. With a smooth bald head and a pencil-thin moustache, he reminded Michela of a rat. His eyes and stance were as calculated as a sneaking rodent. Michela knew it must be Percival; he carried a thick coil in his hand—the whip.

"Now, Michela, get out! Sarah, get up!" Beric said. This was the first time, since they had met this morning, that he had used their names. "Get outside, both of you!"

Simultaneously moving towards each other, Sarah's little feet running, and Michela taking the longest strides she could, the two gripped hands and spun towards the door.

Having received a signal from Beric, Percival let the whip fall from its coil and, with a flick of his wrist, he cracked it, directing it so that the tip touched Sarah on the arm. The little girl screamed and ran faster. Michela kept pace with her. She heard Beric's laugh echo hideously around the great hall. Another joined it, and the sound of Percival's laugh sent chills shooting down Michela's spine.

Intractable tears began to fall down Michela's cheeks. Was this to be their farewell from home?

Michela and Sarah hurried to the carriage, the door of which was held open by a footman wearing Beric's livery. This carriage had belonged to their father. Once seated in the familiar vehicle, they strove to catch their breaths. Michela's cheeks burned from both pain and anger, and Sarah covered her mouth to stop herself from crying aloud.

Suddenly remembering her father, lying in state in the chapel, Michela opened the carriage door. How could she leave her home—his home—without laying him to rest in the proper manner?

She came face to face with Beric.

"Out of there! Both of you! Before you enter my protection, we'll get a few things straight, and you'll learn some obedience! Come on! Get the brat out of there!"

Michela and Sarah stood like two convicted felons facing an executioner.

Stepping closer to Michela, Beric spoke with bridled fury through clenched teeth. "You'd better get that mighty, invincible look out of your eye, girl. Cast your stare at my feet! Don't glare at me like that, as if I'm beneath you! Next time you see me, you'll both curtsy! I'm your lord, as of today. You're chattels, furniture, creatures, vassals, things."

Michela felt his saliva splatter her face and knew he was relishing his wrath, further establishing his domination over them. Still feeling the heat of his hand on her cheeks, Michela lowered her eyes. She did not feel strong enough—not now—to test his limit. And she had Sarah's safety to consider.

Beric was silent for a few seconds, as if surprised that she had conceded. "Now hear me," he said, "you'll think about obedience, obedience, obedience! All the way to Clifton Castle you'll remember that I expect total subordination. You do what you're told, when you're told, and how you're told!"

Michela looked back into Beric's eyes, and, with a snarl, he barked, "My feet!"

She obeyed.

He shouted as though commanding an army, "Twenty-two miles lie between here and Clifton Castle; you'll walk every mile of it! It'll take you around four hours if you don't dawdle. Turn left from the gates here, and at the first crossroad, you take the road marked 'to capital'."

Michela stared at their persecutor, feeling confused. She did not believe he would make them walk twenty-two miles. How could they leave their home, driven out like peasants? She wanted to shout for her father to come. Was he dead? Was this a dream? Had he really died? Was Beric just part of a nightmare, the monster in this dream? No, it was reality; their father had died. She had seen him—cold and still—lying in the coffin, had sat beside him all night. She remembered touching his face and wanting to kiss him, but could not, because he had felt so cold.

Michela drew a breath, forming words to ask Beric about her father... did she dare? Stepping backward, she appealed, "Please, Lord Beric. I... we wish to mourn our father, to bury him..."

His face changed color, and his cheeks puffed out. His face reminded Michela of the gullet of a turkey turning red and purple. Pointing his finger towards the open gates, he shouted, "What'd I say? Obedience? This is the last time! What you're told, when you're told, how you're told!" His voice rose a decibel: "Percival!"

She felt Sarah's hand snatch hers, and the girl pulled her toward the gates. The whip cracked, but thankfully Percival was not close enough; he had been supervising the work of the slaves.

Together, Michela and Sarah left the home they had known all their lives and began to walk on the road toward Clifton; the opposite direction led to the village of Rayburn, where there might have been familiar, sympathetic faces. Michela wondered if they could not go somewhere other than Clifton. Where could they go? Perhaps they could cut through the woods and circle back to Rayburn. But would they be safe there? Beric would likely search for them if they did not walk to Clifton.

Another thought crossed Michela's mind. She wondered that Beric allowed them to walk, unaccompanied, all the way to his castle. Such a thing was unheard of. Young ladies did not walk the countryside alone. She glanced down at her boots, feeling somewhat relieved that Beric had commanded them to dress in traveling clothes. Turning as they reached a bend in the road, Michela's heart leaped into her throat; two men-at-arms marched behind them, their bayoneted rifles resting on their shoulders.

Walking faster, the sisters reached the crossroad and followed the signpost reading "to capital—via Clifton."

Two

Sarah clenched her teeth and strode on like a soldier, having seen the two men trailing them. Her hip hurt where she had landed on the hard floor; her arm smarted from the burn of the whip; her boots pinched, and her nose still did not feel as though it belonged on her face. She tried to remember the words of one of her favorite songs, but her mind seemed blank.

The hot springtime sun soon made the two girls pant from the heat and from thirst. Their long-sleeve black dresses were too hot for this foot journey and the pace slowed. Michela glanced backwards to see how close the two guards were. They had slowed their march to compensate. Relief coursed through Michela's veins. Such a small thing, but so important to her that Beric's men-at-arms kept their distance.

Slowing even more to a comfortable walk, the girls caught their breaths. It was not as if walking were foreign to the sisters; they had often traveled on foot with selected servants, making day-trips around their father's estates, visiting friends and helping the needy by delivering baking and provisions from the great castle stores.

A large gray hare ran across the road between the girls and the guards. Dropping to their knees, the two men, clutching the rabbit's feet they wore around their necks, muttered an incantation to drive away what they believed to be the spirit of disaster. Then, together, but not in sync, they muttered, "Bad luck, it's bad luck! Oh ----------! Not in the daytime. A rabbit, a rabbit! The sun's shining! We're undone! We'll fall into to great harm!"

Michela turned away from the men as they then made obeisance in the direction of the wind. She made use of their superstitious anxiety to place more distance between them. Having been tutored by a Christian monk, both Michela and Sarah repudiated the countless superstitions considered normal in this supposedly enlightened era.

The shock of the morning's events had not fully registered yet, and Michela allowed a little to seep into her conscious thinking. There were cooks and servants and under-servants, grooms and gardeners, butchers, candle makers, men and women of twenty other occupations, all, dismissed. Beric had been furious to find there were no slaves he could claim.

Where had all the bewildered, loyal employees gone? Not along this road, she hoped! No, after Beric's display of despotic power in confiscating the castle, they probably would head in the other direction. She hoped someone would plead their cause and rescue them. But who would think of them, or remember them, now?

While Michela was pondering the ramifications of Beric's seizure of the castle and contents and his claim to their guardianship, Sarah's mind was moving in a different vein. Looking behind her to see that the men still kept their distance, Sarah began singing...

"Stepping stones, stepping stones, ev'ry trial is a stepping stone. Stepping stones, stepping stones, leading to God's Heavenly Throne.

"Sing with me Michela," she insisted, and sang another round. "Please sing with me." She sang solo again.

The singing was erratic, not completely in tune. Michela forgave her though, as she knew it would be difficult to sing and walk while feeling traumatized.

"Why not?"

"I've got a headache."

Sarah's bottom lip dropped and she walked in silence. Then, slowing down, she said, "I feel sick, and I'm tired. Remember, Michela, we hardly slept... we didn't sleep. Then Lord Beric came." She shook her head, looking at the ground. "I'm thirsty and very sad. If I sing, it isn't so awful, Michela. I'll die if I can't sing."

So Sarah sang the refrain, over and over. Michela asked her to sing something else, but Sarah said, "I want to sing this because that is what we are walking on each time we have a trial—it's a stepping stone. Just like Brother Reuben said. Our trials are stepping stones and take us to better things. He said we get closer to God every time we go through a trial and keep our faith."

Brother Reuben. Michela wondered what had happened to her father's old chaplain. She walked in silence as they neared a small settlement. Both girls knew they were out of their father's province and had entered the province of Clifton. The small village was like any other, except the faces of the women and children staring at them as they passed between the crude cottages and huts were sad and sober. Smiles were as rare as gold sovereigns would be in a place like this.

A quad of loitering youths frowned at the small group and Michela remembered the jewelry she wore under her black dress. Her right hand bore three rings and she felt sure the men had seen them.

Sarah ran ahead to the village well and drank copious amounts of water, splashing the cool liquid on her face as well. While Michela waited her turn, she saw that the two guards now stood close to the well, between the youths and the girls. She held her head high, but did not look at the guards. They were both their prison-wardens and bodyguards, she realized.

Sarah resumed the walking and the singing, and Michela wondered how far they had come—how far was it now to Clifton Castle? She realized she had not concentrated on the countryside, or the journey, its length, its direction; there was no direction. Not any more. Horsemen came from behind and the walkers moved aside. Wearing the livery of Clifton Castle, the men rode on without acknowledging the travelers.

Another cross-roads was reached and there were four markers: one to Rayburn from where they had come, the through-road went to the capital, and the other two to provinces Michela had never heard of. How little she knew of the geography of their country, Rompavia. How little they had traveled. How protected they had been in their castle home and province, how little they knew of the world.

Sarah began singing again, but it became slower and slower until she ceased.

"You don't believe the song, Michela, do you?" she asked.

"I'd rather not talk about it, Sarah."

"But you have to keep faith, Michela."

"Yes, Sarah, you do."

"I mean *you*, Michela. Don't you believe that this trial will prove out to be a stepping stone?"

"Not right now, darling," Michela replied as pleasantly as possible, "I can't see for all the mud around those stepping stones you sing about. But don't mind me, I have a crowd of things on my mind." She looked behind and saw that the men were only a few yards away. "Keep singing. We mustn't slow down."

But Sarah did not sing again. A few yards further, she stopped walking. Moving off the road to the grassy edge, Sarah flopped down in the shade of a thicket and laid her head on a log.

"Sarah, we can't rest here..." Michela saw that the men-at-arms had stopped as well. They unslung their rifles, and one began peeling off his jacket.

"I'll carry you on my back," Michela whispered in her sister's ear. "Climb up on the log." The thought of stopping in this abandoned countryside with two nameless soldiers was not Michela's idea of good sense, especially after such recent trouble with their militant master.

Sarah perked up. Climbing up on the log, she hitched up her dress and sprang on Michela's back. Throwing her arms about her sister's shoulders, she clung to her neck.

"Lean forward a little, Sarah, and don't strangle me so."

Michela staggered; then, as the road became more level and sloped slightly downhill, she walked easier.

The pace slowed to that of a tortoise. *But at least we're not standing still,* Michela thought. Her back ached, as did her neck, and she knew she would not be able to carry Sarah much further. Perhaps she had carried Sarah for two miles? Or three? If only they had slept last night. But how could they sleep, when all they had wanted to do was sit close by their father's coffin and imagine he was sleeping and not dead?

Sarah's head slumped on Michela's aching shoulder. Gritting her teeth, Michela continued.

Horses' hooves sounded out. A cavalcade, still reasonably distant, approached on the road ahead. Michela told Sarah to let go and stand up. It was not a lady-like thing to be doing, walking with a seven-year-old girl on one's back. Sarah hobbled off the road, stepping gingerly over a narrow ditch. She leaned her forehead on the gnarled trunk of a tree, and then eased herself to sit. Gathering her dress around her knees, the child hid her face in the black fabric, weeping tumultuously, her shoulders heaving from the sobs.

Michela also stepped over the ditch, and stood in the shade, almost as if she wanted to conceal the sorrowful, abandoned picture Sarah painted. She stood stiffly, watching the leading mounts approach. A standard she did not recognize fluttered in the light breeze. Nor could she identify the uniforms of the many men-at-arms. They wore blue jackets with white crisscross sashes, blue caps, and black trousers. *How little I know about such uniforms,* she thought. Until today, she had believed her father's footmen wore the same livery as every other soldier in the kingdom; uniforms made of fabric of a golden-tan shade. Beric's men wore red.

How sheltered their lives had been. Apart from walking to the village and well-planned, chaperoned excursions about the estates, their father had kept them in the castle. When guests or visitors came—always invited or by arrangement—Michela and Sarah had been commanded to remain in the west tower where they had slept all of their lives. From the battlements, they had watched the comings and goings, but were never invited to be part of them.

Michela stood stiffly as the company slowed, now scarcely moving.

Beric's men stood to attention, saluting.

The captain touched his cap, acknowledging Michela, but it was as though she did not see him. Behind the horses marched numerous foot soldiers, keeping time with each other even when practically stationary. Slowly the company moved on.

The captain frowned at Beric's men-at-arms on foot. Usually men in such a position—in such uniform—rode horses. He wondered if they had mounts near by. Slowing down, he looked back at the two young ladies on the roadside. Both were attired in black dresses flocked with the dust of the road, their hair mussed a little, especially the younger one, who looked exhausted. She was crying, and the captain felt, for a brief moment, that he stared at his own young daughter, who was the same size and hair coloring.

The captain's frown deepened as his eyes scanned Michela, knowing she was no peasant, but a lady, one he had never seen before. He looked for some signal from her; was she in need... or danger? She stood straight like a queen, and as her chin tilted a little, he realized she was very beautiful. With a stare across at Beric's men again, he filed a picture in his mind of this peculiar encounter. Beric's two guards stood to attention, not moving.

When the last foot soldier disappeared around the distant bend in the road, Michela sat down beside Sarah. She arranged her dress over her legs in a lady-like manner, but wished she could stretch them out. The two men had moved away, retreating a little, in the direction they had come, looking at the distant bend as if they expected a return. Michela wondered why they were upset. Was it that the company was so large? Perhaps they were from another province and should not have been here? One thing she was sure about: Beric's men were staging a heated discussion about the troops.

Closing her eyes briefly, Michela felt some relief in resting in the shade. Then the thing she dreaded happened—the two men came closer and closer.

"We can't stop," one said, "we must move on."

"We are resting," Michela contradicted, "you may go on if you wish."

The guard gave a wry smile. "It is you, lady, what has to move on, all of you." Pointing to Sarah, he said, "All means her too—all her blubbering, all her sniveling and whining, and all of her silly songs!"

The other said, "Look, Lord Beric is going to come along in your fine carriage and if he's seen the king's company, he's going to be mad at us if he thinks they saw us, what with us being off our mounts and you being on the road too; it kinda looks strange, you know. The turn-off to the castle is just around the next corner. We need to be well on that road before Lord Beric comes."

Michela rose from her rest and shook out her skirts.

"You'll have to carry me again, Michela," Sarah said tearfully, "I can't walk another step."

Michela allowed Sarah to climb on her back again, wondering how far she herself could last. She made it just past the turn-off. The road began to rise steeply and Michela found it impossible to continue. She dropped to her knees, and Sarah flopped down beside her.

"If y' give me one of them rings, I'll carry y' sister," the larger guard offered.

Michela was very reluctant to give away a ring at this stage; she hoped they could be used to pave their future to a better home than that of Beric's. She recalled the guard verbalizing his fear of Beric.

"If you carry my sister, we will not speak to Beric of having encountered the king's company."

The soldier whistled while the other laughed loudly.

"I'll carry y' sister until the castle is in view, then she has to walk."

Michela guessed that it was far beneath one of Beric's men-at-arms to be caught carrying the 'brat' that his master acquired from a debtor's settlement.

Sarah was hoisted into his strong arms and carried like a child. Feeling somewhat eased in this trek to what she now imagined to be the abyss of misery, Michela increased her pace to keep abreast with Sarah's new legs. The other man marched behind.

Grinning, Sarah's bearer increased his pace. The child was feather-light to the strong man, though he felt admiration for the lady beside him who had carried her sister so long. She was a tough one. She was taking two steps for his every stride, still holding herself like a lady along this pot-holed road. "Beric's going to have his hands full making this lady grovel," the man hissed to his peer who marched at his side.

The road twisted and turned, rose and sighed, but Michela was aware of only one thing, that she wanted to keep pace with this primate who carried her sister. She could not let him get ahead, she could not! Her heart pounded in her chest and her throat suddenly felt dry because her breath had to be taken in gulps through her mouth.

Then suddenly, the man pulled up and stood Sarah on the road. "Over the rise is the castle; if we keep on like this, we'll be there before Beric."

They could not 'keep on like this'; Sarah was exhausted and so was Michela. It was all the older sister could do to lend Sarah support to walk, and keep going herself. However, they did arrive some five minutes before Beric, for which the two men-at-arms were pleased.

Their venue was of no interest to Michela, she had enough to do to support Sarah, who leaned on her, limping, in great pain. As in a dream, they walked under the arch, through the open gates and into the courtyard of their new home.

Three

"Come on, come around the back and I'll have them get'cha a drink," the largest guard urged.

Mindlessly, the exhausted girls followed. People everywhere stopped and stared. But Michela saw no one; she was too tired and too intent on supporting her exhausted sister. They sat where the guard directed, on a bench in a large outer chamber, which looked to Michela like the scullery. The other man had not followed, but had stayed to chat with comrades at the gate.

A strange-looking woman took Michela's attention for a few seconds. Dressed in dark purple garb that was almost black, the woman was counting rabbits' feet into a container while mumbling a chant of exoneration. The feet were fresh, and the woman's hands stained with blood. Michela had never seen a witch, but servants had described such a woman and Michela herself had read about people who delved into the occult. This woman fulfilled every mental concept Michela had of a witch.

"Michela... please... my boots. Take them off," Sarah gasped, leaning back on the chunky chopping-table.

Michela knelt down and unlaced the boots, then attempted to remove one. Sarah cried out in pain, her face paling to ash, her hands clutching at Michela's shoulders. She yelled, "No, no, don't. Leave them!"

Sickened, Michela sat back on her heels. She herself had been too preoccupied to recognize Sarah's predicament. Michela had recollections of these boots, which had once been her own. The boots had always pinched fiercely at the heels. In the current pessimism of her reflections, Michela felt sure that Sarah would never want to sing about 'stepping stones' ever again. This was no road to heaven, and Michela worried that there was worse yet to come.

Sarah's blistered, bleeding feet had swollen in the tight-fitting boots, and Michela had no idea how to get them off.

"They're ill-fitting, are they?" the large guard asked as he took in the situation. Sitting beside the weeping Sarah, he pushed her to sit upright, saying, "Drink this; drink it all." With his paw of a hand at the back of her head, he put the clay tumbler to her mouth and poured in the liquid he had brought for both Michela and her sister. She swallowed and spluttered, then swallowed again, choking on the fiery fluid. Some trickled out the corners of her mouth, but the man persisted until it was all gone.

Ignoring Sarah's gasping and coughing, he knelt on one knee, staring at the boots. Drawing his razor-sharp dagger, he slipped it into the gap at the front, deftly slitting the leather until he had to twist the blade to cut it through at the side, making the incision all the way down to the sole. Concentrating deeply, he carefully repeated the slice of destruction to the other boot.

Peeling back the leather, he freed first one foot and then worked on the other. There was nothing Michela could do but watch this bear of a man tending to her sister in what she had to admit was an impeccably gentle manner.

Sarah crumpled forward against his broad shoulder, gasping in pain. The leather was bloodstained from the raw flesh at the back of Sarah's heels. Drawing a deep breath, Sarah shuddered and fainted.

"Here, hold her, and I'll fetch Calla."

Michela quickly took the guard's place, but lifted Sarah around so that she, herself, could sit on the seat. She cradled Sarah's head and spoke in soothing tones of love.

A large woman, equal to Beric in shape and size, padded out to the scullery. Taking one sweeping look at both Michela and Sarah, she said, "You both need cleaning up, feeding up, and putting to bed." She clicked her tongue as she inspected Sarah's feet. "That'll take a week's rest, or more, I'm telling you!"

The smaller man-at-arms who had walked with them, rushed around the corner of the yard, calling, "Beric's arrived, Jack, and he's yelling for us and the Raynor girls. He wants to know why they wasn't waiting out front for him."

Jack collected Sarah in his arms, saying to Michela, "You have to go, Miss, and it be best if you keep your mouth shut... don't say one word! You don't want him to take it out on the kid, do you?" Looking down at Sarah as she opened her eyes, he said, "Don't snivel, or you'll be in for it; one thing Beric can't abide is whimpering or blubbering. And remember, round here, his bad breath can mean death! So try to sweeten him some. He can be tolerable if he's beholden to."

Michela followed Jack around the outer perimeter of the castle outbuildings to the front. It was strange, but now that she knew a name, Michela felt as if she had found some kind of ally in an 'enemy' soldier called Jack.

Carriages, wagons, carts and horses that Michela recognized from Rayburn were drawn up behind the carriage by which Beric stood. The courtyard seethed with activity the same as at Rayburn Castle, though now in reverse. Slaves and servants—having walked from Michela's home—began unloading the plunder.

"There you are!" Beric bellowed. His eyes rested on Sarah's blood-red heels before searching for Michela.

Stepping to Jack's side, Michela suddenly remembered Beric's command to curtsy. She would have swept him a flamboyant one, but something in his eye caused her to drop him what she imagined to be a polite but servile bob.

Beric's beady eyes darted back to Sarah's feet, then to Jack's face, and across to Michela, asking, "You walked? Every mile?"

Remembering Jack's warning to keep quiet, Michela bit back her reply.

Jack gave a side shake of his head toward Michela, saying, "She walked every inch, Lord Beric, that we made sure; and she had to carry this 'un on her back, half the way, it was."

"Did you see the king's company?" Beric asked, stepping closer.

"King's company? What would they be doing in Clifton Province, Lord Beric? Ha, I'm glad we were out of the way before they saw me and Andy without our steeds!"

Sarah wriggled weakly, twisting her head away from Jack's shoulder to look at Beric. The sight of him so close caused her to close her eyes and go limp in Jack's arms.

"She's collapsed again," Jack said, "dun in, she be, Lord Beric. Calla said she'd clean them up and put them to bed. At your leave, sir."

"Calla can have that one, Jack. I'll take the other to Lady Elisabet."

"No!" Michela cried. Her deepest fear was coming to life; they were going to be separated. She caught Jack's frustrated head shake. The man backed away with Sarah in his arms, and Michela felt sick enough to faint herself.

"No?" Beric bellowed, stepping closer to her, his fists clenching and unclenching.

She braced herself, believing he would strike her again. Then, in a less harsh tone, he said, "You have a bruise."

Michela could only stare at him in bewilderment.

"On the side of your face." He pointed.

"I bruise easily," Michela replied, remembering the extra force she had felt in the blow from the back of his hand as it clouted her cheekbone.

"Follow me, Michela," Beric commanded, at the same time beckoning two guards. He strode across the courtyard to the main door of his castle.

Acting outwardly like a mindless puppet, and inwardly hating herself for it, Michela followed Beric. The guards fell in behind her. Her brief encounter with Calla gave her a boost of confidence; she instinctively knew the woman would tend Sarah like a child of her own. And Jack had proved himself. He had been protective of both Sarah and her. Perhaps there were some human beings at Clifton. Maybe they weren't all monsters like Beric.

Trailing a few comfortable yards behind Beric, Michela took no notice of the corridors and turns he took; it was of no importance. She was being separated from her sister. Since their mother had died six years ago, Sarah and Michela had never been parted—even for one night.

Stopping before a door that blocked the corridor, Beric waited. A guard hurried to open the door. It was locked.

Strings of oaths, curses, and profanities such as Michela had never heard flew out of Beric's mouth. As if struck by a volley of attacking bats, Michela recoiled away from him, but he did not notice. Beric's explosion of verbal garbage consumed him with violent passion. He blasphemed while hammering with both fists on the door, claiming amidst expletives that those brainless buffoons who had locked the vile door would come to a hideous end any second if the said door were not opened before now!

Michela's hand flew to her mouth as if to halt the loathsome language, most of which she could not comprehend. When Beric turned, she could not look at him, but cowered away as if he had struck a blow at her very soul. He began walking back the way they had come.

"Fetch a battering-ram! That door will never be locked on me again!" He turned as the sound of bolts being shot echoed along the corridor. The door swung open.

"Lord Beric, but if you had sent word; if we had known you were coming... this way... but... you wish to speak with Lady Elisabet? But I shall proceed you..." With that the small wizened creature, dressed in the livery of a footman, scuttled off up the corridor.

"Do I have to be announced to my own quarters?" Beric bellowed.

Michela followed Beric as he strode after the disappearing man.

Up a stairway, along corridors; Michela became breathless. How could Beric walk so fast up stairs when he was so grossly overweight? Ignoring bowing footmen, servants and attendants, as if they all were invisible, Beric strode on. The wizened man ahead made sure every door was open, and finally, he announced the lord of the castle to a huge lounge on the third floor.

Ladies were all a-dither to curtsy. Lord Beric strode to a door. Pointing to the guard behind Michela, he waited. The man opened the door and then returned to the outer corridor.

The largest bedchamber Michela had ever seen opened before her tired eyes. Then Beric stood in the doorway, eclipsing most of the room from Michela's view. There was the sound of a large quantity of water splashing.

"Why, Beric, dear. How nice to see you've returned so soon. Did it all go according to your plan? Did you bring me a little something?"

Stepping into the room, Beric turned and beckoned to Michela. She followed him, conscious now of the carpet beneath her travel-stained boots, and the opulence of her surroundings.

"Elisabet, this is Michela. My wife, Lady Elisabet," Beric announced, his eyes upon the blue foam surrounding his wife in the large oval bath. The room smelled of an exotic perfume. Knowing it was expected, Michela curtsied. She felt numbed, unable to look up. To be in a lady's bedchamber with the husband present was improper; and the lady was in her bath!

"Make the girl presentable; I want her at table tonight. You know what I expect. And you may have all of the jewelry you discover on her person," Beric said, grinning at Michela's downcast face. His lips folded back and his teeth bared, making his ugly features more repulsive than ever. "Do something to hide the bruise on her cheek, Bet."

"We will go… on Monday?" the lady in the bath asked.

"It'll depend on that bruise," Beric replied, then added, "Have her watched; she's got rebellion in her eyes. Take her to see Neda and discover her weaknesses for me.

"I've matters to see to… I've not been able to find the one person I need… he must have left Rayburn before I arrived."

Striding across the room to a small door, Beric disappeared. Michela's eyes focused through the open doorway and she realized it was a communicating door—Beric had gone into his own bedroom.

Lady Elisabet stared at Michela for a few seconds, then ordered her to undress. Michela refused without speaking, standing aloof, and turning to stare at the curtain billowing out from the wide balcony doors. Sunlight beamed from high windows, making Michela's untidy hair dance with gold. Trying to avoid the peripheral view of her eye, Michela nevertheless captured an impression of Lady Elisabet's slim body being assisted from the bath and the women attendants drying her. The lady lay on a couch and a young woman applied copious amounts of a strongly perfumed cream to her body, massaging it with expert hands until the cream was absorbed. That the heinous Lord Beric had such a beautiful young wife was a great surprise to Michela.

A diaphanous negligee was wrapped around Lady Elisabet's exquisite form as she rose from the couch. She cast her attention on Michela. Holding her hand out, she commanded, "Give me your rings."

Michela obediently removed two, saying, "I would like to keep my mother's wedding ring, Lady Elisabet, please."

"Give it to me. Let me see it."

Michela hesitated before drawing it from her finger. Set in gold, three flawless diamonds faceted prismatic colors around the room.

"Give me the rest of your jewelry."

Michela did not move until she saw Elisabet gesture to the women attendants. All three stepped toward her and Michela knew she was lost. Bowing her head, she reached to unhook the top hooks at the back of her dress. One by one she gave the necklaces to the closest woman. Without speaking, she turned her back, waiting for her dress to be undone. Slipping it to a dusty heap on the floor, she extended her wrists so that her bracelets could be removed. A diamond-studded gold belt at her waist was also unclasped and given to Elisabet.

"Finish undressing her and put her in the bath." Elisabet said. "Search the hems and seams of her clothes, then wash her hair."

Tears of humiliation pricked Michela's eyes, but she forced them into oblivion as two women, ignoring Michela's efforts to care for herself, obeyed their mistress's demands. Against Michela's will, she found the silky warmth of the bath water relaxing her. The heady aroma both soothed and calmed her.

Elisabet's attention was on Michela's jewelry. She examined each piece as the women brought it to her. They retrieved a small treasure-trove from the wide seams of Michela's petticoats. In the process, her clothing was cut to shreds.

"You have a sister," Elisabet's voice cut into her repose. "What happened to her?"

"Sarah is with a woman named Calla."

"With Calla? Why?"

"Her feet are injured; she cannot walk. Calla is caring for her."

"How did it happen—her feet?"

"We walked from Rayburn. It's twenty-two miles and Sarah's boots were not made for walking so far."

"Have her brought here," Elisabet commanded, speaking to a woman-servant. "Make a bed-chamber ready for the pair."

Michela brightened. Then she realized Elisabet's stratagem; she wanted Sarah's jewelry. Both carried jewelry on their persons, sewn into their petticoats. This was a precaution taken by the aristocracy of the time, an insurance against pillage of their property and personal poverty. Michela wondered how many people knew about this procedure.

Sarah was not going to be separated from her! Michela surrendered to the warmth of the bath and the attention of the woman. Sarah was going to be brought to this part of the huge castle, and they would share a bedchamber.

Four

Lady Elisabet was in a temper, but unlike Beric, she managed to control herself. She did not threaten or swear. She simply asked many questions of Michela as the latter lay on the couch receiving a body massage from hands that made her feel weak from relaxation, yet also rejuvenated.

From the returning servant-woman's halting narration, Michela learned that Sarah had been located and carried to the prepared bedchamber. Calla had already bathed her, bandaged her feet and dressed her in an outsized servant's frock. Sarah's clothes were missing and the child wore no jewelry.

So much for my assessment of Calla, Michela chided herself bitterly. She thought of Jack and wondered whether he shared the booty. *But Sarah is here! Sarah is near.*

"Sarah had jewelry?" Elisabet asked, "Or was big sister the sole treasure-house?"

"My sister had jewelry," Michela admitted, knowing Elisabet would find out anyway.

Elisabet spoke with antagonism, "I can't believe Beric! He should have had your jewelry confiscated before you left Rayburn."

To Michela's embarrassment, a tall thick-shouldered man—behaving like a privileged slave—was freely admitted to the huge bedchamber. Speaking to him, Elisabet commanded, "I want Calla and Jack questioned, Hannibal, and tell Lord Beric that the child had jewelry and that it's all missing—there's not a locket or a ring—then report back to me."

Elisabet's attention was again on Michela.

"Is it true that your father never had you presented at court?"

"Court?" Michela repeated, wondering why she should be presented at a hall of judgment.

"The King's court," Elisabet said, "No. I see you do not know about court. Then it is true; you didn't travel out of Rayburn?"

"No, Lady Elisabet."

"And you weren't present when your father had company?"

"No."

"He kept you both like prisoners," Elisabet declared, adding, "you'll be as ignorant as church-mice. And about as useful." The woman paced across the room, then asked, "You have no relations, even distant?"

"No, Lady Elisabet."

"Then Beric's right. There's nothing to fear," the lady concluded.

She paced again, back and forth across the chamber, frowning at Michela as though something did not add up in her conniving, calculating mind. "You're no slug, Michela, either mentally or physically; what did you do with yourself all day... every day?" Without waiting for an answer, she asked, "You ride, don't you?"

"Yes, Lady Elisabet, but not often."

"You walked around the estate. Once a month you did a complete circuit. And your sister had lessons... a tutor, Samuel James, wasn't it? He taught her, having taught you all he knew..."

Michela did not answer, but wondered who had given Beric's wife so much accurate information.

"You read a lot, Michela; what else did you do with your time? You didn't sew—your clothes were made by a tailor; though dreadfully dull in color, they're well put together. You didn't embroider, or do any handiwork, did you?"

"I learned to spin fleece," Michela said, sure that Elisabet believed her to be useless.

"Spin? Yes, you spun wool for shawls and gave most of them away. How boring.

"Your father sought no suitors for you. As far as the world outside Rayburn knew, Lord Raynor lived alone in his castle with no heirs."

"Father did not believe daughters to be of note..." Michela began.

"He could have gained a rich dowry from the right baron," Elisabet persisted. "You're not plain, Michela, not at all... dressed in something... bright, or even plain white, you could be quite startling. That black is pitiful!" She narrowed her eyes asking, "So, why were you not married off?"

"Perhaps, Father felt he could not do without me," Michela said. She felt deliciously relaxed and quite unthreatened. Elisabet had been angry, but not with her and Sarah; it had been directed at Calla and Jack and the missing jewelry. In comparison with Beric, Michela felt safe with Elisabet.

"What are you saying?" Elisabet asked sharply, causing Michela to start. The older woman stepped to the side of the couch, asking, "Why did you say that? In what way could your father not do without you?"

"I was both clerk and scribe," Michela replied. Seeing the confusion on Elisabet's face, she explained, "I kept all the books, Lady Elisabet. Samuel James taught me all he knew about accounting and bookkeeping. It took nearly all my time."

"You did *all* the book-keeping; kept *all* the accounts? How much did you do? Who helped you?"

"I did all that had to be done once the inventory was written. Father would not allow me to go to the storerooms or the cellars or barns, but all the records and figures written in the castle office were worked by my hand. From the taxes to the accounts and records on the estate, also all orders for goods and replenishment of stores. Father brought me all the figures."

"My sources knew nothing of this," Elisabet said. "It must've been kept secret." She smiled suddenly and said, "Beric is furious about the clerk at Rayburn having left the castle without his knowledge... he said it was believed your father did the accounting himself; but we knew he could not have, not without help. Beric said that the handwriting in the documents and books was not Raynor's. No one had been able to give Beric the name of your father's scribe." She paced across the room again before directing a command to a woman-servant, "Fetch our evening gowns; and then we'll have our hair dressed."

Michela watched, fascinated, as Elisabet's hairdresser transformed the lady's long black hair into an elaborate style such as the girl had never seen. While another woman expertly applied cosmetics to Elisabet's face, the hairdresser transferred her attention to Michela. Watching the woman in a large mirror, Michela felt strangely detached. *Is this my hair that is being fashioned so expertly?* she mused. She had obtained glimpses of visitors and guests who had come to the castle, and she had thought how very grand they had looked. Now, her own hair was being arranged in this elegant, feminine way. Some plaited around the crown of her head, the rest wound on hot rods into neat coils, then released to hang in glossy ringlets. If Michela had not been so fascinated, she would have grown tired.

Then the make-up artist plied her mistress's cosmetics to Michela's face. The bruise was camouflaged with cream and powder, and it disappeared completely under an application of pink rouge. Another layer of powder was added. Then eye-color—kohl— and lip-color were applied.

Michela felt she stared at a complete stranger and the 'stranger' stared back. It made her feel unnerved. Elisabet laughed at the serious set to her ward's face.

"Yes," she said, and her voice became serious, "Michela has disappeared. We've a new lady here now. What name shall we give you?"

"I'm very happy with Michela."

"Beric says you must be called by a different name. What are your other names?"

"I was named Michela Elizabeth Alexandria."

"Elizabeth is too much like mine. We'll call you Alexandria. It's much like the king's name. But that won't matter; you won't be meeting him. I feel sure he won't be asking to meet you."

"The king?" Michela asked, wondering.

"King Alexander."

"I've heard of him, as everyone has," Michela said, knowing that her knowledge was limited to the gossip of servants in her father's castle.

Elisabet stepped towards the door, beckoning with her ringed forefinger for Michela to follow, saying, "Come, we've a few minutes before we're expected at table. We'll discover your destiny, Michela, and how it will affect mine—and Beric's."

Michela found herself swept along behind Elisabet, moving down, down, down, into the very depths of the castle itself.

The chamber they entered was dark and murky with the smoke of strangely sweet but musky-smelling incense. Many images filtered past Michela's deliberate blockade of indifference. Around the top of the walls, skulls of animals of different shapes and sizes had been fixed, with the occasional human scull amongst them. Star shapes, arrows, crosses and circular symbols were painted on the ceiling. A tall container filled with rabbits' feet stood near the central table, which was scattered with many articles Michela had never seen before, some about which she had read. A massive crystal orb, looking as though it would roll off at any moment, balanced on a special stand, and there were bowls containing acorns, colored stones, teeth, feathers, keys of all sizes, and other incidental 'good-luck' charms.

"This is Alexandria, Neda. I want you to find out how Beric and I may control her. Beric wants to know her weaknesses. Her main weakness is most important, Neda."

The thin woman behind the table peered into the crystal ball. In a single glimpse, from her side of the table, Michela saw a distorted picture of the painted face. She remembered this woman's bloodstained hands counting out rabbits' feet, and she shivered. Looking away from the ball, her gaze rose to view the skull of a goat and she closed her eyes, wishing herself anywhere but in this horrible chamber screaming with bizarre objects symbolizing witchcraft and sorcery.

"It won't be easy," Neda said in her slow deep voice. "She won't cooperate. You won't even be able to change her name..."

"You don't know that," Elisabet snapped.

"Ah, but I do. And I'll show you..." Neda gathered up a pack of Tarot cards. Bringing them around the table, she spoke to Michela, saying, "Shuffle these for me, Alexandria, and choose one from the pack."

"No," Michela replied, and several reasons for her refusal formed sentences in her mind.

"Why not?" Elisabet demanded. "Neda can show you your future in the cards."

"God alone knows my future," Michela said firmly. "I believe in God." She felt a pain in her chest, which seemed to chill her heart. Yes, she did believe in God, but she was unable to give encouragement and comfort to her little sister this afternoon when it had been so desperately needed. *What faith do I have—if any?* she wondered.

"Ah, but which god do you speak of?" Neda asked.

Feeling both intimated and out of place, Michela did not reply.

"We're wasting time. Beric will want an answer at dinner," Elisabet said. "We have to go up in a minute or two."

Stepping close to Michela, Neda stretched out her claw-like hand toward the girl's face. Expecting to be scratched, Michela closed her eyes. The woman smelled repulsive! A slight prick at her hairline was all she felt. Neda had plucked a single hair. Curiosity forced Michela to watch this young witch.

Placing the long hair in the pack of cards, the woman shuffled them herself. The card found near the hair was placed on the table. Neda exclaimed about its significance, muttering that their subject had lost a great fortune but would find it again, then the woman expertly separated and laid out the rest of the cards. Elisabet joined Neda at the table to watch, and Michela's vision of the cards was obscured.

Michela's mind flew to her little sister and she wondered how she was faring. Did God care about her? Did He even know where they were now? Did He know she was in this pit of evil? Had they trusted God in vain? Michela felt tears pricking at her eyes. If only she could pray, if only God would come to her aid now.

"You'll have to find out what's treasured by her, what's dear to her. A bribe... no, a threat may be necessary, but she'll do as you say if you find the key. Already she's been somewhat subdued..."

"What, then, is her weakness?" Elisabet persisted.

"It's not in treasures... no, not a bribe..." Neda said, her concentration on the arrangement of the cards, "It's in human flesh... I see blood..."

Neda, her eyes half closed, rushed around the table and stared into the crystal again. Lifting her hands up, she cried, "I see blood, I see blood!" Peering into the crystal she said softly, "It's blood from a child's feet... the secret is in the child." Her voice rose to a triumphant pitch as she declared, "It is revealed to me. Threaten to bruise the child, and you will control Alexandria!"

A feeling of sickness rose within Michela's being. She remembered Neda in the scullery with blood on her hands; Neda would have seen Sarah's injured feet. How easy for this witch, knowing Michela's tender and earnest concern for Sarah, to turn this into a triumph for herself.

Neda still gazed into the glass, crying, "I see blood, more blood…"

"Whose… blood?" Elisabet asked.

Neda shook her head, then spoke, "It's either the child's or Alexandria's. It will be revealed, but not now, not today."

"Then we must test your revelation, Neda," Elisabet said. Laying a piece of paper on the table, she turned to Michela and said, "Take up the pen and write for me. I wish to show your handwriting to Beric. That way, your claim as clerk and secretary of Rayburn shall be established. Did you hear what Neda said, Alexandria? Do you wish Beric to have your sister whipped, or worse, because you won't obey us?"

Without replying, Michela moved to the table and took the quill from its stand. Dipping it in the ink, she asked, "What would you have me write for you, Lady Elisabet?"

"You'll write for me, in your most formal handwriting, word for word as I dictate, 'I, Alexandria Elizabeth Clifton, am ward, servant and vassal of Lord Beric and Lady Elisabet. Their wish is my command.' And sign it, girl."

Blinking away rebel tears, Michela did as she was told. In a moment of outrage at Elisabet's dominance over her, Michela did not sign the paper with her name, but wrote 'Girl' as Elisabet had inadvertently commanded.

Having stared at the flowing script and the signature, then at Michela, Elisabet smiled a satisfied smile. She rolled the paper and said, "We shall go to dinner, girl, and Beric shall be pleased with us both." She looked like the cat that had captured the mouse she had hunted for all day long.

Five

Escorted by two of Elisabet's ladies-in-waiting, Michela stepped to the place indicated at the main table. She stood between the two, awaiting the arrival of the lord and lady of the castle. Soft conversations circulated the hall, but everyone's focus was upon the main entrance, in anticipation.

The topic of the conversation was 'Lady Alexandria'—everyone knew where she had come from and all but Michela herself knew the reason Beric required her cooperation. However, no one knew that the reason for the master's delay was the lady's handwriting on a small roll of paper.

Beric was, at present, comparing Michela's writing with that in the Rayburn Castle record books. It matched the writing in the account books as well, and other documents, journals and papers.

"This changes everything," Beric said, "We'll have to keep her."

Elisabet's face crimsoned. "You've never kept a girl before," she said in anger.

"This is not the work of a girl!" Beric said in reply, "This is a clerk, a secretary, an accountant."

"You'll be telling me she is a genius next!"

"Yes, that too. She's done for Rayburn what takes four men, with my oversight, to do here at Clifton. And Rayburn is a larger province than Clifton."

"She had her father's help!"

"Her father has not written in one of these books. Be reasonable, Bet. She can save us four salaries."

"You said she was to be married off, like the rest," Elisabet persisted. Her red lips puckered into a girlish pout.

"She's far too valuable; I'll keep her, and as the sister is the key to Michela's obedience, I'll have to keep Sarah as well. Let's go to dinner," Beric concluded, and his wife knew she must not argue. A great fear surged in Elisabet's heart as she tried to comprehend the depth of change in Beric's attitude toward their new ward.

"Will you still take her to the capital?" she asked.

"Of course. We'll not miss out on our valuable little trinkets, love, shall we? Perhaps, if you can manage her, we'll receive double, just as I did with you, Bet."

"I'll have to see," Elisabet conceded, but her mind seethed with schemes and plots of how she could get rid of someone as potentially dangerous as this 'church mouse' from Rayburn. "And remember, Beric dear, her name is Alexandria. You'll see a tremendous difference in our little Rayburn mouse now, Beric; our ladies worked very well with my cosmetics and perfume."

Elisabet's fire of anger and jealousy in Beric's new evaluation of Michela was further fanned when Beric paused before the table at which their ward stood. Having been announced to the great hall, Beric's 'court' had given him the expected obeisance required as he strode toward the main table. His eyes searched for his wife's two ladies and when he saw the lady who stood between them, he could not believe the transformation. If he had not recognized her partners, he knew he would not have known Michela.

Beric stared for a long time at Michela. Having looked at the beautiful silk gown she wore, then examined the elegant design of her hair, his eyes lingered upon her face. To Beric, she looked like a goddess wearing too much make-up. To his satisfaction, her stare was dropped to rest on the table in front of her. A mysterious shade between blue and green, her eyes were fixed as though upon something far away from Beric's world.

Michela did not look at Beric or Elisabet, but politely curtsied again as they stopped near her. Raising her eyes a little, she stared at a huge tapestry on the far wall. It depicted a conglomeration of animals hunted for game. But Michela did not see the wild boars, or the stags, or the bears; she was thinking of Sarah. How could she protect her little sister and also keep her own identity, and her sanity? It seemed impossible. *And I must not think of Father; I must not think of him. I won't manage to keep my head, if I remember him as I last saw him...* She blinked away threatening tears.

Beric moved on with Elisabet, seating her at one end of the long table. He walked to the other end and sat, calling, "Be seated, and begin." Simultaneously, everyone reached for the food, eating it as fast and as noisily as possible. The previous orderliness turned to chaos. Michela, used to dining with her father on every occasion that there were no visitors or guests, could not believe the furor that ruled at Beric's tables. From where she sat, she could see both Beric and Elisabet, and knew that they, too, could see her.

People reached across each other, talking loudly. Using their hands to break up joints of meat, they stuffed large chunks into already crowded mouths.

Michela looked for the utensils, but there were none. If she wanted to eat, she would have to use her fingers. The lady on her right, whose name she heard as June, slapped a joint of chicken on her plate. Feeling both hungry and disgusted, Michela decided that the former need was the one to satisfy.

The chicken was deliciously tender, and Michela enjoyed baked root-vegetables, fresh beans, and a variety of chunky pieces of raw vegetables and fruits from bowls presented by waiters assigned to each table. Those at the main table had one footman serving each couple. To Michela's relief, servants brought steaming hot hand-towels, one towel to be shared between two, and June indicated that the towel be passed to Michela first.

Desserts were served in a similar manner. Huge round fruit pies—precut into wedges—had daubs of thick cream applied. Michela enjoyed the thick pastry crust; glazed with toffee-like syrup, it tasted delicious. It was impossible to pick up all the contents of the pie, or the slippery cream, in one's fingers, and Michela did not try. She found her eyebrows rising in amazement as people took their plates in both hands to lick them clean. It seemed animalistic to Michela, but in spite of having passed through the worst day of her life, she saw the funny side of it all and smiled. This feeling of mirth caused a thousand other sensations to relieve themselves in the abandoned corners of her mind, and suddenly, she felt close to tears. No longer did it feel like a nightmare; Michela shivered, knowing everything around her was all too real!

A messenger entered the hall and the din subsided a little. But it was not enough to be able to hear what the man spoke in Beric's ear.

The master stood and shouted, "Find it all! All of it! Beat it out of them!"

The messenger spoke again, after which Beric shouted, "They claim you have it all? Bring it here. And have them both brought here! In chains!" Then Beric turned to stare directly at Michela. She felt a shiver run down her spine, although she had no inkling of what Beric had shouted about. After a moment, Beric's attention was back on his food.

A nameless dread made Michela's heart sink. Her thoughts raced as she contemplated escape. But Michela knew her thoughts were grounded in impossibility. *What can I do? Where can I go? I'm trapped here in this castle—Beric's domain. He's my master, and Elisabet is my mistress. For Sarah's sake, I must obey them; she mustn't suffer because of me.*

Again, towels were passed around, and chatter rose to a frenzied pitch. The ladies on either side of Michela talked over her or to those on the other side of themselves. To speak across the table was impossible; it was too wide and one was unable to hear because of the high volume of babble echoing around the hall. People grew merrier and more rowdy. Some folk changed places with others.

Goblets emptied, filled and emptied, filled and emptied and filled. As soon as drinking vessels were emptied, cupbearers filled them again. When Michela sipped from hers, she realized it was some kind of strong wine. Just a few sips made her head spin. She left it alone, deciding she must at least keep her mind clear. Stealing a peek at Beric, she saw that he was drinking deeply, while engaged in discussion with those men on either side of him. Ladies surrounded Elisabet at the other end of the table. *Women dressed up like peacocks,* Michela thought, her eyes taking in their beautiful clothes, elaborate hairdos, and sparkling jewelry. *They're all older than Elisabet... they're at least as old as Beric. However did she come to marry him? It is like a marriage of a swallow and a vulture... yet they seem to agree; somehow Elisabet has gained Beric's approval. He doesn't look down on her. He doesn't treat her like a slave or a vassal, or a thing.*

Michela viewed Beric's table guests with a little more interest. Most of them, she realized, would enjoy prized positions in Beric's castle. Some would be glorified companions and advisers. Others would have exalted positions such as overseer; perhaps one was the clerk, seated by his wife; the secretary and his wife would also be present. She tried to picture the kind of occupation that would suit the person she inspected. It made the evening more interesting, even though she had little experience to back her deductions.

Occasionally, Beric directed a question at a specific person seated at another table; this way, Michela learned some of the people's names. Then, as that person gave their answer, she tried to project what their personality would be like, their very character. *It will be interesting to know if I am in any way right in my assessments,* she mused. *Beric has a very interesting house of cohorts. I wonder if I'll find a friend here?* Michela did not imagine these people were the kind she could ever consider as friends. They each and all seemed to have selfish interests and pleasures at heart. *How do I know this?* she asked herself. *Perhaps it is the way they eat; the way they choose the largest pieces; the way they push and reach over others, and the way they are drinking now to excess.* Michela's experience did not go beyond the castle staff or the villagers and farmers on the estate. Never before had she been so close to people who would be termed as the "upper class." They left her feeling disappointed.

A commotion was heard at the entrance, and guards strode in, following a footman bearing a wooden tray upon which Michela recognized Sarah's jewelry. A somber hush fell over the great hall as the tray was placed in front of Beric. Elisabet swept from her place to his side, her eyes viewing the jewelry with greed. The only sounds were the clanking of chains, the scraping of feet, and the slow movement of several guard's boots.

Some distance behind the tray of jewelry, a man shuffled along painfully, hindered by the heavy chains he wore. His face was bloodied and bruised, his back beaten so that shreds of his vest were embedded in the freshly bleeding mass—Michela recognized him as the man-at-arms called Jack. His only clothing was a long sleeveless vest, shredded at the back and hanging just low enough in the front to be considered decent. She felt embarrassed for him.

Then Calla arrived, having dragged herself along between four guards. Michela felt sick to her stomach. Never before had she seen people in chains, let alone a woman who had been whipped. Blood oozed down Calla's legs. Her simple linen undergarment was in shreds and did not cover her properly. Michela averted her eyes, feeling like screaming in protest. Anxiety rose within her as the reality of Beric's brutality dawned on her.

"Lady Alexandria, step over here," Beric's belligerent voice called, stabbing the silence. Every eye turned to look at Michela as she moved away from her table. *I must obey him,* she told herself. *For Sarah's sake I must obey everything he demands of me.*

"Look at the jewelry, Alexandria; examine it. Tell me what is missing, and describe the pieces to me."

Michela hesitated. Her eyes met Elisabet's and she perceived the woman watching her closely. There were two pieces missing; and her sister Sarah knew each piece as well as she. Elisabet's eyes warned Michela that they would question Sarah. Michela knew that she had to sacrifice both Jack and Calla to save Sarah. But she hated the compulsion. If only she could do something to save these two. Anyone was worthy to be saved from Beric's savage wrath. Michela knew she would plead for the life of a kitten, let alone a human being...

"There are two pieces missing... a necklace... it's a row of rare gray pearls, each fastened to the other by silver links," Michela said, "and a ring. It was a silver ring with one stone."

"The stone?" Beric demanded, not taking his eyes off her face.

Michela kept her eyes upon Sarah's jewelry. "It was a diamond," she said.

"How large a diamond?" Beric asked.

"Very large," Michela admitted, "the largest diamond my father owned."

"Sarah? Your sister wore this ring?" Elisabet asked, her voice incredulous.

"My sister wore no jewelry; it was all stitched into her clothes," Michela answered. Then, remembering Sarah's clothes, she said, "The ring is probably still in its place. It was sewn into a shoulder pad that I pinned in the mourning dress. One would not realize any jewelry was in the pads."

"And the pearls?" Elisabet persisted.

"It was in the other shoulder-pad. Perhaps it is still there?" Michela replied, looking at the lady, her voice hopeful. It was obvious that these two in chains would be further beaten if the jewelry were not retrieved soon. Michela knew nothing of torture, but the idea of something similar entered her mind as she thought of Beric and his tantrums.

Beric sent the two captains away to fetch the clothing, "With the shoulder-pads—make sure the shoulder-pads are there," he commanded.

Low murmuring and fragile conversations followed the departure of the guards. Calla sank to her knees with a moan, and Percival cracked his whip to land upon her bare back, making her cry and struggle to stand again. Several gasps followed the crack of the whip, but all was silent when Beric stood to his feet to see who it was that defied his discipline by gasping about it.

Before the whip crack, Michela had not noticed Percival's presence, and she closed her eyes to block out thoughts of his whip and her sensitive little sister. *I must do all I can to prevent Percival from whipping Sarah,* she told herself.

Michela opened her eyes to view the tormented Calla, whose mouth quivered as she obviously struggled to prevent another whimper from expressing her pain and misery. A sudden sickness rose from Michela's stomach, and she braced herself with one hand on the table. She remembered Beric's violence and his threats. Was it just this morning that she had met this diabolical man? Surely Beric would not have Sarah so severely whipped?

"Our little Rayburn princess finds the chains and shackles a little unnerving, Beric dear," Elisabet said sarcastically, adding, "I wonder how she will find a crows' cage. Have you seen a crows' cage, Alexandria?"

"No, Lady Beric; I... I mean, Lady Elisabet," Michela replied, her mind whirling. She felt both dismayed and angry.

"Then you shall be entertained, dear girl," Elisabet said, while beckoning a footman to bring a chair. "We learn something every day, don't we, Alexandria?"

"Yes, Lady Elisabet," Michela replied, knowing this was true. Without thinking, she added, "Even if the lessons are spurious and undesired, Lady Elisabet, they have to be endured."

"Ha!" Beric said, then belched rudely. He had a comment to make, but with his eyes upon the distant entrance, he swallowed and belched again. The captains strode into the great hall behind a servant who carried the torn remnants of Sarah's clothes. Beric slid his chair aside to give his wife more room at the head of the table beside him.

Beric and Elisabet, their eyes gleaming in anticipation, searched for the two shoulder pads amongst the pieces of black fabric. They were still pinned on the garment, and Beric pricked his thumb in his haste to free them. A string of expletives flew from his cavernous mouth. Michela found herself blinking, but strangely, she was not as horrified as the first time she had heard him swear. Somehow she felt she had let herself down. To accept this man and his foul mouth in any way at all was a self-betrayal.

Beric turned to Michela, commanding, "You had them put there, girl, so retrieve them for me!"

Michela leaned over the table and unpinned both shoulder pads. They were flat, sewn across in rows, as if quilted. It seemed impossible that any jewelry could be hidden in them.

"I need scissors, Lord Beric."

Without speaking, Beric drew a thin sharp dagger and held it to her, handle first. A multitude of emotions ran through Michela, all in a millisecond of time.

A dagger... I could stab Beric right in the middle of his chest, but it would not save Sarah and me... Elisabet would see to that.

I could use the dagger on myself; it would be easy to fall on it, against the table... but how would it help Sarah? No, I cannot; I'm a prisoner because of their threats. My love for Sarah forces me to do as they say...

Michela took the dagger and slit the tightest seam in the shoulder pad. It had been stuffed with kapok, in the middle of which was the diamond ring. While Beric and Elisabet poured over the huge jewel, Michela slit the other pad and drew out the pearl necklace. The gray pearls were exquisitely rare, and obviously priceless. Beric drooled as his eyes examined them.

After a few minutes, Elisabet lifted the pearl necklace carefully from Beric's large hands. Moving her chair away, she knelt at his side, saying, "Fix it around my neck, Beric. Do you not think they go well with my gown?" Lifting her hands, she covered up the diamond and sapphire necklace she wore. It had belonged to Michela and she wanted to keep both of them.

With amazingly deft fingers, Beric placed the necklace around his wife's long neck, fastening the catch at the back. With equal swiftness, he undid the diamond and sapphire necklace. Looking up at his ward, he asked, "Would not the Rayburn princess like a reward for her cooperation?"

Beric had never before given anyone a reward or a gift, save his own wife. Every mouth in the great hall dropped open in amazement. Beric wanted to please his new 'ward,' not just to bully her! It was unbelievable.

"Alexandria would prefer this ring, would she not?" Elisabet said, pulling off Michela's mother's wedding ring. The three diamonds glittered enticingly into Michela's stare. She had given up all hope of owning this ring again. Words failed her as Elisabet snatched up her hand and pushed the ring on to one of her fingers. With just as quick an action, Elisabet retrieved the necklace from her husband's outstretched fingers.

Six

The feeble but ominous clink of chains entered Michela's conscious thinking. She felt both Jack and Calla's shame as if it were her own. Why should these two suffer so much, while Beric, the instigator of the whole saga, was victor and conqueror? If only she could do something to help Jack and Calla. Beric was permitted to steal the jewelry, but not these two—they had to suffer. She looked at the two human shapes, chained not only with physical chains, but also with defeat and degradation

Boots sounded out, accompanied by a new noise. Everyone watched the procession as it came closer and closer. Two 'crows' cages' had arrived. Made of heavy iron, they were wheeled right into the great hall and close to the main table. Without ceremony, the two prisoners were seized, their shackles unlocked, their chains removed, and they were bodily stuffed into the ill-fitting prison-cages, their arms and legs poking out through the bars.

A loop at the top with a chain attached told Michela that the chain was for hanging the cage up somewhere. But why were the cages called 'crows' cages', she wondered? A sick feeling caused nausea to rise again as her mind followed the trail to the obvious conclusion. Calla and Jack were to be hung somewhere, and would eventually die, and become—crows' food. It did not take much imagination to know that the crows would start on Jack's back first and there was nothing he could do about it. If only she could say or do something to interrupt the gruesome nature of Beric's abhorrent intent.

Anything is worth a try, she thought, as an idea came to her racing mind. Pulling the ring from her finger, and kneeling at Beric's side as she had seen Elisabet do, Michela placed the ring in front of the master of the castle. She did not speak, but bowed her head. *I want to pray, please God, I want to pray, but I cannot. You are not here; You are not in this place. How can I pray to You? But please, God, please, if only You could hear and help.*

Beric looked at the ring in amazement, and then stared at Michela. He looked up at his wife, his eyes searching for the diamond and sapphire necklace.

Elisabet felt wild fury rise in her throat. This creature from Rayburn had designs upon Beric, her husband! All she could see was her husband, taking the necklace from her, giving it to another woman. In that instant, she could have killed Michela.

"Give her the necklace, Elisabet... the one you have in your hand."

"Please, no, Lord Beric," Michela cried. How much the jewelry meant to these insatiably greedy people; it dominated their thoughts. "I don't want the necklace... or the ring, Lord Beric."

"What she wants is her freedom!" Elisabet said, her eyes blazing with malice. "She wants her freedom from you, Beric dear. That is how she rewards us for taking her in."

"No, Lord Beric," Michela countermanded, raising her head to look him in the eye.

Beric asked the question that Elisabet hated to hear, and no one could believe he asked, "What do you want then, little Rayburn princess?"

Michela, remembering his anger of the morning, and not comprehending the change in Beric's attitude towards her, dropped her eyes. She wondered if she dared ask, then knew she must. Everyone was waiting.

"It is not for myself that I ask," Michela began.

"What do you want, other than your necklace or your ring or your freedom?" Elisabet interrupted, "Perhaps you want your sister released?"

Michela thought of Sarah. How good it would be to have her set free... but where could she go? Where would she be safe? There was nowhere to go—no one to go to. Michela believed Sarah would not survive if she were not near her sister.

"Tell me your request, Alexandria, and I'll do my best to fulfill it!" Beric said, but smiled cynically as if he might refuse.

"My request is for Jack and Calla," Michela said "You have ultimate power in your hands, Lord Beric, power to grant life, or death." She paused and waited, hoping her words would sink in through his large thick skull. "Please, Lord Beric, my request is that you spare Jack and Calla, that you show your power by granting mercy." Looking up at him, she saw the fury in his widened eyes, and bowed her head, expecting him to strike her. She remained on her knees, not flinching, scarcely daring to breathe.

Beric's face changed all the colors of the rainbow. His cheeks puffed in and out, he sniffed and coughed and banged his fists on the table. Then he stared up at the sneer on Elisabet's face, and it was as though something inside him cracked. He shouted at his wife, "The girl is right, isn't she? I've never granted mercy, never spared anyone before, and why should I—but why should I not?" As if reading the questions on Elisabet's face, he asked, "How can I do this for these traitors? Won't they just turn on me?" Beric turned his attention back to Michela.

"If I was to grant your request, Alexandria, I would be freeing two thieves, two unfaithful servants; how could I be sure that they would not turn on me and rend me like hogs would rend their wounded master if they had the chance?"

Michela thought of several retorts. Was not Beric himself such a thief? Had he not stolen the jewelry in the first place? He thought himself to be wounded, but how many others had *he* wounded? But he was right; both Calla and Jack were unfaithful; they had betrayed their master by stealing from him. Michela decided to keep her mind upon the main issue.

"Perhaps, Lord Beric, you could exile them from your province without recommendation."

"Bah!" Beric said, and spat across the table. "It's too good for them!" He sat thinking, and no one dared to speak. Not even Elisabet. She was dumbfounded beyond thinking by Michela's request, and equally speechless to hear her husband sanely discussing the possibility of allowing Calla and Jack to live.

"Captains! Arrange for these two cheats to be transported over the border... out of the kingdom; do it now. Get them out of my sight before I change my mind!"

He waited for the cages to be wheeled out before he looked across at his wife's ladies. His shout made everyone jump, "June! Bertha! Take Lady Alexandria to her room and lock her there. She's to be treated carefully, as you know, but also as one who can't be trusted." He looked at Michela's white face, her downcast eyes, and repeated, "Very manipulative. One who can coerce me into showing mercy is indeed one to watch! I want her in the castle sanctum, first light in the morning. Make sure our princess sleeps well."

Michela rose without looking at either Beric or Elisabet. She did not have the heart to thank them, nor did she want to let them know that she felt she had achieved a great victory. Beric had conceded; he had granted clemency when his evil being cried out against mercy, desiring slow painful death for his former employees in the crows' cages.

As she walked with June and Bertha back to Elisabet's quarters, Michela wondered if God had heard her feeble 'prayer' after all.

Perhaps if he had heard a prayer for such as Calla and Jack, he might hear a prayer for Sarah and herself? If no sleep could be gained this night, Michela made up her mind to pray.

Sarah was deeply asleep in the large bed when Michela entered the room. Although Michela kissed her cheeks and caressed her forehead, Sarah did not stir.

The two ladies helped Michela undress. They combed her hair out before creaming her face to remove all trace of make-up. When her face had been washed and finally creamed again, she donned the nightgown they fetched, and climbed into the bed. Then they left the room, locking the door behind them.

Michela went to the window and eased herself behind the drapes. In the same instant, a deep voice called from the castle gate, "Midnight, and all's well. Midnight, and all's well." It reminded her of home, and the deep longing for everything to be as it was just a few days ago swamped her, threatening to drown her. Dropping to her knees, Michela allowed the floodgates to open. She smothered the sound of her sobs in a small linen hand-towel. Nevertheless, all the grief of the past two days flowed out like a torrent. For over an hour, she could think of nothing but that her father had died in a fall from his horse and had left them forever.

Tears of disbelief, sorrow and disappointment that her father had left them with such a guardian as Beric washed her face. Another hour passed, and then Michela felt the deep need to pray.

Oh, Lord, I'm so sorry. I've not trusted you. I've felt that this trial is a bottomless chasm, a place with no path, a meaningless void. But it must be, as Sarah says, a stepping stone. Help me, Lord, to see each trial as a stepping stone. Thank you for Sarah's faith. Help me to encourage her and not dishearten her or make her turn from you, Lord. And please, dear God, help me to protect her... please God, don't allow Beric to harm her.

How long Michela prayed, she had no idea, but finally, when she rose and climbed into bed, she knew that the early fingers of dawn were rising to select the colors that would change the night into day. Her eyes and mind had scarcely closed in sleep when a sweet little voice came to her ears...

"Michela, Michela. Oh, do wake up. I didn't know you were sleeping with me." Sarah's arms surrounded her sister and she kissed Michela's cheeks. "I feel much better, Michela. I hope I can walk before the week is up. Calla said it'd take a week. Hannibal says he'll carry me everywhere I want to go." She looked around the room, now lightning in the dawn, "Did Hannibal bring me here? I remember him talking to me and carrying me, but I don't remember arriving here."

On remembrance of Calla, Michela came to complete consciousness. She wondered if Jack and Calla really had been taken over the border into another kingdom. She hoped they would find a new life, a life in which they did not feel they needed to steal. She wished them a life without people like Beric in it. At the sound of a key plied to the lock, Michela turned her attention to her sister.

"Sarah, darling. You must be obedient and do all you're told. I have to look at the accounts with Lord Beric and we might have to be apart, but I'm hoping it won't be for long." She remembered how Sarah used to sit at the other side of the table, reading, doing lessons, or handiwork while she herself took care of her father's books. It was all in the past. Nothing would be the same again...

June and the make-up artist, with the hairdresser, all entered the chamber. June carried clothes for Michela. Peeling Sarah's arms from her neck, Michela rose and dressed. While Sarah watched with wide eyes, Michela was transformed back into the princess of last night. Instead of an evening dress, she wore a beautiful day gown.

Before she left the room, Michela kissed Sarah again. The young girl declared earnestly, "You look beautiful, Michela, really beautiful. You look like someone else's sister."

Before breakfast was served in the great hall, Michela gave Beric, his clerks and secretaries an overview of Rayburn's record books: journals, accounting books and legal papers. There were a number of bills of promise, signed by various small landowners in the province.

Beric declared himself famished and said they would continue with the examination of the books after breakfast. He seemed in a good humor, but Michela felt too afraid for Sarah to relax her guard.

Elisabet was not at the meal, and for some reason, Michela missed her. Perhaps it was that Beric bade her sit beside him and she received stares and was aware of directed comments from those in the great hall; she felt unnerved. Beric thought her to be more valuable than just a horse, perhaps, but Michela knew instinctively that Elisabet would not be impressed with her husband's attention.

The day passed quickly for Michela. She immersed herself in her father's books. Beric wanted everything explained and Michela wondered who would be placed in charge of the province of Rayburn? Surely a province of such a size could not be left unattended? She would wait patiently for the 'right' opportunity to ask Beric. The day after tomorrow was the Sabbath, and Michela hoped it would be a day of rest as it was at Rayburn. Perhaps she would find the right moment to discuss her home. Maybe Beric would send her back there to continue in the task her father had set her.

~ * ~

The next day followed, a repeat of the previous. Sarah was permitted to read in the library all day. When Michela returned to their room that night, the girl was fast asleep, and after being prepared for bed, Michela prayed. She and Sarah had had only a few minutes together that morning.

But Beric ignored all tradition and religious observance; each day to him was another day, and the only restrictions were those gained by consulting Neda, their fortuneteller. Beric and Elisabet consulted Neda each night, gaining advice, recommendations and warnings for the following day. Michela had no doubts that they believed her voodoo suggestions—as if Neda was a god that spoke to them.

Michela again found herself in the sanctum, seated at the table with piles of books around her. Beric had left her with the clerks and secretaries. She learned that the two provinces were to be combined. Everything would be managed from Clifton Castle. The castle at Rayburn would be used as a storehouse until Beric chose to change its status and install an overseer who would answer to him. In simple terms, Rayburn had been annexed.

Tears pricked Michela's eyes, threatening to run. Unable to blink them away, she dabbed them on her sleeve. The men shifted their feet and coughed uncomfortably as Michela salvaged her emotions.

Later in the day, two hours before they would be expected 'at table', Elisabet sent Hannibal to escort 'Lady Alexandria' to her chambers. After Michela was bathed, massaged, and dressed, Elisabet told her of the plans for Monday. Michela learned that tomorrow's journey and outcome was the main reason Beric wanted guardianship of her.

"Of course, your wonderful, brilliant abilities with the books and accounts have changed Beric's mind about you, Alexandria," Elisabet said, with contempt in her voice. "He was going to have you married off after the test."

"The test?" Michela asked, wondering.

"The King's Test. Surely you have heard of the King's Test, Alexandria?"

"No, Lady Elisabet, I've never heard of such a test."

Michela listened as Elisabet explained. "I was one of the first maidens in the kingdom to take King Alexander's test. We evaded the rules and I took it twice, under two different names. I was sponsored by Beric, who married me after I returned the second time. It was over five years ago that the king and his counselors designed the test to find the king a wife. He seeks a special woman, you see. And he's set a test to find the right one. It's a bit like Cinderella trying on the glass slipper, I suppose. Everything has a legend behind it, I believe. From what I've heard, like myself, very few pass the first stage of the test. In five years, there've been hundreds of maidens who have taken the King's Test. Beric and I are taking you to the capital, on Monday, Alexandria, to take the King's Test."

"What... what do I have to do?"

"Oh, it's very simple. You have to select three gifts from the king out of a number of about thirty pieces. Some of the gifts are fabulous beyond dreaming about. Diamonds from the king's mines—some are larger than the one on Sarah's ring. There are sets of tiaras and necklaces; the jewelry is more valuable than anything we saw before... other than your pearl necklace, which must be one of a kind." She drew a deep breath, concluding, "Beric has already decided what you are to choose."

"Is the king present at the test?"

"Not when you choose your three gifts. However, if your choices please His Royal Majesty, you have to take a second test." Elisabet smiled, enjoying seeing Michela's consternation, "For the second part of the test, I understand, the candidate has to stay the night at the palace... with her chaperones, of course.

"I've been thinking a lot about you, Alexandria, and I'm hoping you'll pass the King's Test; perhaps you might be the one he's looking for?"

"Me? Oh, no, Lady Elisabet. But—I'd rather not take this test. It all sounds... it sounds so... so incomprehensible to me. I don't wish to pretend I'm interested in the king when I am not."

"You really don't get it, do you? You're to be interested in what I tell you to be interested in, Alexandria!" Elisabet spoke firmly. "You won't choose the things that Beric tells you to choose, but you'll listen to what I tell you. I'm having Neda work out what the king is looking for. Neda told me, secretly of course, that you'll be chosen to take the second test and that you'll not return to Clifton, but will remain in the capital!"

A fear of being caught up in something ominous flooded Michela. "Do you know what the king requires for the second test?" she asked.

Elisabet laughed and said, "There's much gossip and speculation about the second test. The most rumored story is that King Alexander believes in an ancient fairy tale and he wants a wife who's able to spin straw into gold. I don't know, Alexandria; we'll have to wait and see. The rumor says that the candidate is shut in a room full of straw for the night, with her chaperons and a spinning wheel." She laughed, adding, "If anyone can spin straw into gold, Alexandria, I'm sure it'd be you."

Michela could not believe her ears. "Spin straw into gold?" she asked, adding, "That's completely impossible!"

"Beric doesn't think so. He believes in the story that King Alexander's ancestor, Queen Katarina, spun straw into gold before the king married her. She was the miller's daughter, her name was Katie before she married the king. Neda believes in a dwarf named Rumplestiltskin who can spin straw into gold, and she thinks the dwarf helped Katie complete the task." Elisabet smiled at Michela's disdain and added, "Beric would love to make an arrangement with Rumplestiltskin. He would find him all the straw he could, of course, and become very rich."

"Beric believes in Rumplestiltskin?" Michela asked, amazed.

"You believe in God, don't you?" Elisabet retorted.

"But fairy tales and fantasy are unreal… God is real. He's the Creator of all the universe, maker of men and all life, alive Himself, eternal, holy, majestic, wise, just and merciful, kind and loving…"

Waving her hands, then placing them on her ears, Elisabet said, "Hush, child. You mustn't talk of such a god. Speak of the devil, but not of a god who is merciful or loving; talk of evil and superstition, but not wisdom or holiness." She shuddered.

Michela felt victimized and hated the feeling. She spoke with vehemence, saying, "Rompavia is full of superstitions and fantasies. Few people have the light and life that God intends. They're all too busy reading cards, and stars and palms and gazing into crystal balls! The superstition in this castle is abominable, Lady Elisabet, and I refuse to be part of your scheme to gain treasures from the king."

"How dare you preach at me and decry my credence!" Elisabet stepped close to her ward, her hand raised. She dropped it, an evil gleam in her eye. "You refuse, you say? Tell that to Beric tonight, Alexandria, little princess of Rayburn! See what Beric will do with your refusal!"

Michela went to the great hall that night with both dread and determination in her heart. She could not eat a bite, and found that just one sip of the wine made her stomach wind into a sickening knot.

It was not until the meal was over that Beric called to his wife—who sat at the end of the huge table, "All is arranged for our journey tomorrow, Bet? Alexandria knows what is expected?"

"She has something to tell you, Beric dear," Elisabet called back. Suddenly all conversations ceased.

Beric's face turned toward Michela and without hesitation she stood. Instead of speaking from her place, Michela moved to the head of the main table. Curtsying, she searched her mind for the words she had been forming over and over all evening.

"You are ready to take the King's Test for us, Alexandria?" Beric asked.

"I'd rather not, Lord Beric. I have no wish to be numbered amongst those who contest for the king's hand," Michela replied, having forgotten her other answers.

"She has no wish to be counted the same as Beric's wife!" Elisabet shouted from her end of the table. With her beautiful gown sweeping the floor, she strode to Michela's side. "What this ungrateful wench has been saying to me, Beric, arguing with me whilst dressing tonight, in clothes we supply her; is that she's not interested in your bid to gain a little more revenue to help feed and keep her and her precious young sister."

At the reference to Sarah, Michela, dropping to her knees, turned her face toward Beric's, pleading, "I... I don't believe in such a test, Lord Beric. But, sir, if you..."

Beric interrupted, "You... refuse... to take the King's Test? This simple test where you choose for me, your guardian, three gifts from the king... your king?" His voice and face filled with astonishment tinged with lightly veiled rage.

"She refuses!" Elisabet said firmly.

"NO! I shall do it... for you. I... just...I have strong feelings against it," Michela said, hating herself for sounding so lame.

"Fetch the child!" Beric bellowed, and several pairs of feet raced to obey.

All of Michela's doubts disappeared at this command. Beric was more depraved than she could ever have imagined anyone could be. She saw that Hannibal was one of those who left the great hall, and she hoped and prayed with all her heart that he would arrive first. Sarah had said that Hannibal had been kind and protective towards her. It was now very late in the evening, and Sarah would be fast asleep.

Michela cast her attention back to Beric. He stood and paced across to the wall. His fists clenched and Michela realized that he was pacing to save himself striking her. They did not want her face bruised—no, she was to go to the palace and perhaps meet the king. Michela realized his obsession with the King's Test. She wondered how many other maidens he had 'sponsored' so he could gain their chosen treasures.

Beric's boots were the only sound in the great hall. Everyone waited the arrival of 'the child'—and Michela knew that everyone expected to see Beric's fury. She waited for him to turn her way.

"Please, Lord Beric, forgive me. I will do everything—anything— you ask of me."

It appeared Beric was deaf to Michela's concession. He clicked his fingers and gave a strange signal. A footman disappeared and when Percival came in just a few seconds later with his whip in his hand, Michela wished she had never spoken against anything Elisabet had asked of her.

Then Hannibal entered, with Sarah in his arms, still half asleep.

Michela would have run to her, but felt herself grasped on either side. Then the men released her, standing close, forcing her to move forward so that she was locked against the table.

"Stand the child down," Beric said, and turned to Michela. "We have a policy here at Clifton, Alexandria. I've told you before: you do what you're told, when you're told, and how you're told. To argue back or refuse is the worst offence; one has to take the punishment for such disobedience."

"Stand the child down," Beric repeated, and all eyes turned toward Hannibal.

While Hannibal obeyed, placing the small figure clad in her thin nightgown to stand on swaying feet, Michela grappled with the two men, trying to turn around. She desperately wanted to go to Sarah, but they spun her back around to face the table, pushing her forcefully downwards. With a sickening crack, her forehead hit the table.

"Michela! Michela!" Sarah cried. She would have run to her sister, but Hannibal held her arm firmly.

Raising herself, Michela saw her small sister standing in front of the huge slave, Hannibal. Percival was close to Sarah, the whip unfurled, ready to use it at his master's command.

To her consternation, Beric rushed to Michela's side and peered at the growing lump at the top of her forehead near her hairline.

A stream of curses and expletives flew from Beric's mouth as he saw the bump on Michela's head, which was darkening and growing larger.

At the sight of the bruise, Elisabet blurted, "Sarah will not be whipped, Alexandria. If you'll agree to do everything you're told, Sarah will be spared."

Elisabet looked at Beric as she spoke, raising her pencil-thin eyebrows.

"Please, I will do anything, only, please don't whip Sarah," Michela said.

"She questions me! She defies my authority!" Beric said, stamping his foot. He sat in his chair, staring at Elisabet.

"You seem to both hate and love our new ward," Elisabet commented.

"The girl is impossible—she needs to be taught that I am the final word! I'll not be usurped in my own house!" Beric shouted, and slammed his fist down on the table. "The child will be taken below, to the dungeon. She'll stay there until we return. If Alexandria questions me again, I will send word for Sarah to be whipped! Take her below—now!"

Michela clutched at the table and Elisabet supported her, also preventing her from attempting to go to her sister.

All eyes turned to watch Hannibal as he lifted Sarah into his arms. She did not cry out or resist and Michela watched them leave the great hall with a large escort of guards. Beric's voice came to her reeling mind.

"Get some sleep. I'll send the doctor and Neda up to see what they can do about that bruise. Perhaps the King's court will believe the truth, that it was an accident and happened when the lady fell." Beric drank from his goblet and held it to be refilled. His eyes followed Elisabet and Michela as they left the great hall.

Seven

The carriage in which Michela, Beric and Elisabet traveled held some comfort for the grieving girl. It had belonged to her father and she had traveled around the estate several times, just last winter, enjoying its protection from the cold weather. Now, in closing her eyes, she could savor the memory of being in the carriage with Sarah and her father. However, every time she opened her eyes and saw Lord Beric sitting in the seat across from her, Michela's short solace shattered.

Neda had announced on Monday morning that the day was a disaster, unfit for travel. A comet had appeared in the sky in the night and Neda seemed to think this was a very bad omen. The earliest they should travel was Tuesday, the next day, but even this would have to be confirmed. Neither Beric nor Elisabet questioned Neda, but cancelled their travel plans. When Neda suggested that Michela rest all day Monday, Elisabet said, "I'm suspicious of Neda. I hope she hasn't used her position for the comfort of our ward."

However, when Neda spent time with Michela, applying an anti-bruise cream to her forehead, Elisabet said, "That makes me feel better. It's obvious that the girl bruises easily, but she did strike herself a nasty blow."

Michela had dared to ask Elisabet to talk to Beric and gain permission for her to visit her sister before they left. It was with both thankfulness and apprehension that, soon after dawn, she was escorted down to the dungeons, having been told that Beric had granted her request.

The cell in which Sarah was confined was a small annex off the end of a large torture chamber. Michela inched past a large table-frame containing a brazier in which hot embers burned ominously. A number of branding irons and other instruments lay scattered on the table. Although the dungeon was murky with smoke, it was warm.

The huge chamber was hung about with chains, instruments, racks and cages—devices Michela had never seen before, nor did she have any idea as to their purpose or use.

Several prisoners, not daring to complain for fear of further torture, were bound and penned around the walls. Michela's heart grew heavier and heavier.

Upon reaching Sarah's cell, Michela was thankful that her little sister could not see any other prisoners from her cell. Hannibal had fixed a blanket on the bars at an appropriate place, blocking Sarah's vision.

Hannibal sat outside the small locked cell, talking to Sarah. He had promised to bring her whatever she asked for, if it was possible for him to find it. Already her cell glowed from the light of half a dozen brightly burning candles. Michela could see fruit of several kinds. Other food in a bowl was being shared by a hoard of greedy rats, climbing over each other to feed. Hannibal had brought several books that Sarah had been reading by the light of the candles. It seemed he had time and heart to pander to her every wish.

"I be here while you go to capital, mistress. Elisabet go too, and she not need Hannibal; I take care of princess's sister. She have no one to fear. I look after her real well for you."

"Thank you, Hannibal," Michela said, feeling a little better about having to leave Sarah.

Sarah declared in a trembling voice, "I'm sure no dungeon has been so comfortable as Hannibal has made this one, Michela."

"Promise me, Sarah; promise me you will keep singing, at least in your heart," Michela said, as they entwined their fingers through the bars. To Michela's concern, Sarah gripped her thumb in her small hand as she had done when she had been a baby. Tears flooded Michela's eyes and seeped down her cheeks.

"I'll sing, Michela, if you will too."

"If we sing your song, Sarah, we can imagine we're singing together, even though we'll be apart. We'll try to believe that this is just another stepping stone, won't we?"

Sarah's face lit up at her sister's reply. "Oh yes, Michela. I've been reading to Hannibal and he said he has never been read to before." Then Sarah's face dropped.

"What is it, darling?"

They moved closer together.

"I want to read the Bible to Hannibal, but he says the library curator doesn't have a Bible. And look, all the books are in dreadful disrepair. Father would never have allowed it. I want them to look for our Bible." Suddenly switching the subject, she asked, "God does know I'm down here, Michela, doesn't he?"

"Yes, dear, God knows."

Sarah released her sister's hands and reached her arms upward. Bending, Michela hugged her sister closer to her, wishing that the bars were not between them.

"Do you believe, Michela? I mean really believe? You aren't just saying it to make me happy?"

"No, darling. I must say how sorry I am that I let you down. You were right; you must keep believing; if all we have is faith in God, real faith, then we have everything we need. I have been praying, every night since we came here to Clifton; and I know God will be with us wherever we are... even when we're apart."

"Sometimes I don't feel him," Sarah said in a small voice, as if she had committed a heinous sin.

"He has said he will never leave us nor forsake us," Michela said, adding, "no matter where we are; he is there. I do not always feel him, Sarah," she admitted, then added, "I sometimes think that God cannot be here in this evil place, but if he said in his Word that he is everywhere, then we must believe that he is with us. It's when we believe, and trust him, we really feel his presence..."

"Yes, you're right," Sarah said. "There's nowhere anyone can hide from God and that must mean I can't be hidden from him either." She looked around at the candles and said, "God is with us when it is light... and even when it is dark, he's still here."

"Yes, darling. So we will keep singing, won't we?"

"Stepping stones? I'll try, Michela, if you'll promise me that you will sing it too."

"Yes... together."

"Then before you go, Michela, sing it with me now?" Sarah asked, and broke into song, "Stepping stones; Stepping stones, ev'ry trial is a stepping stone. Stepping stones; Stepping stones; leading to God's Heavenly Throne."

Because Sarah had asked, Michela joined in. Her voice was more mature than Sarah's and of a perfect pitch. The sweet sound of it was like a visible ray of hope, shining in one of the darkest places in the kingdom of Rompavia.

"I look after little Sarah... you must go, Lady Alex," Hannibal urged. "Master be mad if you late leaving in carriage... and if he mad, he punish you by punishing little Sarah."

Michela kissed her sister, saying, "When I return, Sarah, you will be released from here," She wanted to add, "I promise," but the words would not come.

"I take care of little sister, and it be only today; I hear the master say you come back tonight. I watch over Sarah for you," Hannibal promised, following Michela up the steps.

Michela felt determined not to cross Beric in even the slightest matter. Sarah must not be whipped. Beric kept his word regarding any punishments. Calla and Jack were the only people in the history of Clifton Castle to be pardoned from a death sentence or any other punishment, so June had told her.

~ * ~

After almost three hours' travel, the carriage halted outside a large inn. Michela was ushered inside, between her two guardians. Beric demanded a private table and breakfast to be served. Michela had little appetite, but forced herself to eat a small amount, knowing they still had so far to travel. Almost three more hours. How could she bear this amount of time in the carriage with nothing to look at but Beric and Elisabet?

Wine was served, but Michela could take no more than two little sips. It was bitter to her palate. She wondered how her guardians could drink it with such enthusiasm.

"You are such a finicker, Michela, Alexandria... there I go again, will I ever get that stupid name right? We should have chosen something shorter and more suitable. Drink up, for goodness sake, Alexandria. The gods all know, we'll need every bit of strength for concentration when we get there."

Once back in the carriage, Beric and Elisabet scoured their memories for information regarding the palace and the test, to pass on to Michela. As they reminisced about their many visits, Michela learned all that was expected of her—what to say and what not to say.

Elisabet revealed that Beric had sponsored eleven girls before Michela, not counting the twice that Elisabet had come for the King's Test.

"This is the thirteenth test, Alexandria," Elisabet said. "Neda fears that it will be disastrous, but she could not find a distinct prophecy. I did not want to come along this time, but Beric said I must."

Michela did not speak, but her quick mind told her that hers was the fourteenth test Beric had brought a girl on. *Not that it matters; Elisabet might contest that I'm the thirteenth girl, but then she said another girl came twice... as she did. I'm so glad I don't have to depend on numbers to make me feel secure. Oh Lord, thank you for coming with me. It's a stepping stone... please, Lord, help me believe it's a stepping stone and not a continuing trail of despair.*

"Neda told you the name of the new contact at the palace, did she not, Elisabet?" Beric asked.

"Yes, it's a woman named Alfena, but Neda said it's tricky to communicate with her... she conducts her work in secret. We must wait for the right sign from an attendant. Neda said that there's been a prohibition placed on occult activities, but she didn't know why."

"One of those pompous advisers we met last time, I expect," Beric said. "They want the king to be sole authority. I suppose King Alexander hands out the omens for the day." He yawned rudely, and then turned his attention to Michela, who smothered her own yawn, making not a sound.

Beric commanded, "Yes, keep your little mouth closed, Princess, unless Bet or I tell you to open it. If you hear me count, it will be the number of strokes your sister'll receive when we return home. Understand?"

"Yes, Lord Beric."

To Michela's concern, Beric drew out a small but very solid pistol from inside his jacket lining. She had seen one just like it; it had belonged to her father.

Beric grinned at her, saying, "Yes, it's a handy little widget, isn't it, Princess?" Flicking the barrel-catch open, he checked that it was, indeed, loaded. He fixed the safety catch and placed the weapon on his knee. Reaching into his jacket, he pulled a larger pistol from the other side. Fingering the metal with undisguised admiration, he checked again that the bullet was in its place. Then, with a twirl of each, he returned the weapons to their hidden pockets beneath his armpits.

The carriage drew to a halt, but Michela doubted they had arrived. She could still see the countryside through the small window. There had been no sign of a city. Beric opened the door, calling, "We're at the Avingworth Lookout, are we? We'll show our ward what she's going to."

Michela did not miss the boastful note in Beric's voice; neither did Elisabet. The latter was provoked; her husband behaved as though he enjoyed taking this maiden, this chattel, this vassal, on a journey; he behaved as though it was an adventure, not a connivance!

Elisabet decided she enjoyed Michela more when the girl provoked and inflamed Beric. This quiet, compliant ward was exactly what her husband appreciated. *I'll have to agitate her into disobedience,* Elisabet decided, *I must take every chance to make her refuse him...*

Taking Beric's outstretched hand because she was afraid to rebuff him, Michela walked obediently beside him to the brow of the hill. Just across the road was a tall tower atop which king's guards could watch over the whole city of Avingworth, and monitor all movements in and out.

Houses, multi-storied buildings and networks of alleys and streets all seemed to lead to a focal point. Michela drew her breath. Across the megalopolis valley was the most amazing sight she had ever seen. At first she did not realize it was the royal palace, she was so overwhelmed.

"It is amazing!" she exclaimed as she took in the dozens of towers and spires, thousands of glass windowpanes reflecting like facets of jewels. Tier upon tier of palace: terraces, balconies and beautiful outer stairways, columns, pillars and gardens.

"Perhaps it will become your home," Elisabet suggested optimistically.

"Oh, I could never live there," Michela declared, having forgotten her mental pledge to keep her tongue quiet.

"We don't want you to live there," Beric said, "You're very valuable to us now, Alexandria."

"Valuable?" Elisabet queried, her voice climbing a pitch higher as she added, "For what?"

"The books and accounts," Beric replied, then seeing the anger on his wife's beautiful face, he added, "My dear, you're being tiresome. Just because we have a clerk and not a chattel? A secretary and not a vassal? Perhaps the journey has been too much? Shall we finish it?" He took his wife's arm and began to walk back to the carriage. "The city takes a little time to navigate, and if we're not there before one o'clock, I feel afraid that we'll not be on our way home before sunset."

Michela stole one last glimpse of the palace, and then followed the couple to the carriage. *Beric is so unpredictable,* she thought. *He can flare into a temper in an instant, but he can speak so nicely if he wants... almost like a gentleman. It's like he's two different people. One violent, the other, almost bearable.*

Michela sat forward on the seat, again looking out the small aperture as the carriage was maneuvered through the city streets. The driver took a by-pass to the palace and Elisabet, looking out the window on the other side of the carriage, chatted about various buildings altered since they had been there the previous year.

Eight

Beric was in a foul mood! His ire was obvious to all, and Michela knew it would be all the more visible to those who did not see him every day. She was sure that Elisabet was used to Beric's tantrums. Elisabet did not even blink at Beric's insulting vocabulary.

Stomping around the room, Beric said, "Nothing's gone as we expected. The rules for the King's Test have been changed. Why we weren't informed I'll never know!"

"You've attended the palace here on several other occasions, Lord Beric," an official replied, stepping backwards at the sight of Beric's angry face. "We... we didn't expect you to sponsor another maiden, sir..."

Another man joined the discussion, saying, "You've married one unsuccessful but beautiful contestant, sir, and we understand you possess many of the king's gifts..."

"Out! Out! Get out!" Beric shouted, stomping towards them and slamming the door behind them. He immediately opened it again, and called, "Get me a copy of these new rules! Fetch them here now!"

One of the officials stepped back into the room. "The credibility and eligibility of the contestant will be subject to confirmation too," he explained. "Six months ago, a 'maiden' came to take the King's Test and she passed the first. But before she took the second, it was revealed that the maiden was a young widow; she had been married and had a child aged two. Neither married women—nor widows of any age—are eligible." The official stared at Michela, adding in an undertone so that only Beric and Elisabet could hear, "Certainly no unmarried girl who is not a virgin should apply for the King's Test."

The other official, breathless, arrived with a sheaf of papers and handed them to Beric. "When Sir Chezney is able to attend you, he'll explain what's expected."

Page by page, Beric and Elisabet read the new rules, the latter obviously struggling to comprehend the meanings of the legal terms on the papers.

"So, little princess, they have to examine you and discover all of your secrets," Elisabet said in a disparaging tone. She ignored the attendants at the door of the room to which they had been shown. "Perhaps they'll discover you've had a love affair or two."

Michela did not comment. She sat on the edge of the plush couch, taking no notice of either the opulence of the spacious chamber, or of the stares of the statue-like footmen. Beric sat, engrossed, again reading through the seven pages of the new rules.

A man was announced to the chamber: "Sir Chezney; Adviser to King Alexander and Steward of the King's Test."

Michela rose and curtsied simultaneously with Elisabet while Beric bowed.

"We meet again, Lord Beric," Sir Chezney said, his mouth twisting in a cynical way. "Not for the same reason, I hope?" His eyes flickered over Elisabet, whom he recognized from previous visits. Then they alighted on Michela. She did not meet his gaze, but stared at the wall behind him. Sir Chezney looked around to see what this candidate was looking at. He frowned and looked back at her.

"We'll go to an office where we'll ask some questions of your nominee, Lord Beric. You may, after all, be on your way home before sunset. We do not allow every applicant to take the King's Test—as you will have seen by the new rules. Come, follow me."

Michela, flanked by her guardians, followed Sir Chezney to the office. Michela had been warned to be silent; her guardians would do the talking.

Once seated, Chezney took up a sheaf of documents and handed them to a scribe. They appeared to be preprinted forms that were to be filled in as the questions were answered.

"Your full name is Alexandria Elizabeth Clifton," Chezney said, reading the paper previously given him. He looked up at Michela and asked, "What is your proper name?"

Michela looked across at Beric.

"The name you were given at birth?" Chezney persisted, then added, "Come now, we all know that Lord Beric is your guardian and that your name is not Clifton."

Beric's face flushed as red as beets. However, he knew himself to be cornered and he had to tell the truth, "Her birth-name was Michela Elizabeth Alexandria."

"Her father's name?" Chezney asked, gesturing for the scribe to write down the answers.

"Lord Raynor—he died last week," Beric said.

"Lady Michela's birth-place?" Chezney asked.

"Rayburn Castle."

The questions continued and Lord Beric answered them truthfully. Never before had such questions been asked. Every candidate had been accepted without questioning and permitted to take the King's Test unchallenged.

Michela and Elisabet were escorted away.

~ * ~

When they were reunited with the now jittery Beric in the reception room, he had decided to abandon the project. Speaking to the official, he said, "I have to be back in Clifton urgently. Tell Sir Chezney that we couldn't wait."

To Beric's surprise and indignation, the official told him he must wait for Sir Chezney to attend them again before they could be dismissed. Although no guards stood at the door, Beric did not dare defy the official and try to leave. His status as a castle lord and baron of the kingdom was at stake. Beric hated the impasse. He was no longer in control. His anger turned on Michela.

"Don't sit there like a drooping wall-flower! I haven't started counting yet, Michela, so do not look as if I have!" He would have said more, but Sir Chezney entered the room.

"You'll be pleased to know that Lady Michela Elizabeth Alexandria Raynor is eligible to take the King's Test. She shall take it tomorrow morning."

"Tomorrow?" Beric bellowed, having forgotten himself.

"You'll be shown to a guest apartment and will have attendants delegated to you. Anything you require will be brought. The evening meal will be provided for you in a dining room adjoining your apartment."

"We'll take your leave, Sir Chezney, and return to Clifton. I have very important matters to attend to."

"Then Lady Elisabet will remain as chaperon for your ward," Sir Chezney said with finality in his voice. "There's no more important matter in the kingdom for your ward other than His Majesty's test, is there?" He looked directly at Michela as he said these words. She lowered her eyes and did not reply. Chezney, greatly intrigued by this young lady, avowed to himself that he would find out all he could about her.

"Perhaps Lady Michela may take time this afternoon to familiarize herself with the rules, Lord Beric. I trust you have a good journey home. Will you return for your wife and your ward, or do you wish us to return them in a Royal Carriage? With Lady Michela's gifts, and an escort, of course."

"I... I... but... I'll consider it. Perhaps, if it's only tonight, perhaps we'll stay, but just tonight."

"If Lady Michela passes the first test, she'll be required for a second night, Lord Beric; surely you remember this condition? It has not changed." Sir Chezney smiled at Michela, but she did not look at him. His eyes flickered as he wondered what this candidate was thinking, and he said, "Who knows? Lady Michela may even pass the second test. Then she shall have her dream come true... she'll be closer than anyone has ever come in the quest to marry King Alexander."

Michela felt her heart thud in dismay and she colored at Sir Chezney's words. Anger and resignation mixed within her, making her feel helpless. Her eyes lifted to meet Chezney's and she perceived he was watching her closely.

"The heart's desire of every young maiden," Elisabet said, her voice coated with a smooth sweetness, like honey. "How very wonderful, dear Alexandria, if you are chosen above all others."

Michela turned away. She felt hot and bothered, and a new feeling encompassed her. The make-believe of it all embarrassed her. "Excuse me. I need some air," she said, and stepped across to the open glass door where a balcony greeted her. The view was breathtaking, but her thoughts were with Sarah and she silently sang the words of their song, praying that Sarah was also singing.

Stepping Stones? she wondered. *How can this experience be a stepping stone?*

Within minutes Michela's short respite ended, and they were shown to their guest quarters in the palace.

Elisabet's attention was upon gaining information about Alfena's whereabouts in the palace. Now that they were installed in a guest apartment, Elisabet knew it would be easier to move about and make herself known.

Beric dropped to a couch in the one sitting room, shared between three bedchambers. His bedchamber was the other side of Elisabet's, whilst Michela's opened off the sitting room. To be staying in a palace guest chamber, with a small army of attendants to cater to their every wish, was of great pleasure to Beric.

"I want a bath," he declared, "and a masseuse to attend me."

Preparations began immediately to take care of this request.

"Michela and I would like to visit the library," Elisabet said. Taking a five-pointed star-shaped brooch from her traveling chest, she pinned it to her dress. Michela was not quite sure, but she felt that several pairs of eyes among those of their attendants noticed Elisabet's brooch. Two young ladies, dressed differently from the servants who wore uniforms, followed them.

With a sinking heart, Michela walked with Elisabet behind the footman who led them to the library. *Superstitions and evil... I did not feel it until Elisabet put on that brooch. This palace almost had a friendly feel until then. It must have been the spaciousness and the warm furnishings... it had an atmosphere of welcome...*

"I should have brought June or Bertha; oh, why am I so thoughtless and stupid?" Elisabet berated herself while Michela browsed along the shelves in the huge library. Discovering a Bible, Michela carefully lifted it from the shelf and took it to the table near the windows. Within seconds she was engrossed and was almost deaf to Elisabet's announcement that she was leaving her in the library while she herself took a walk.

Elisabet had not returned and Michela realized that the sun had disappeared—suddenly, it seemed—behind distant hills. The library was four floors up in the palace and as Michela stared out across the valley of Avingworth, nestling in the deepening shadows, she felt entranced by the beauty of the scene.

A feminine voice broke into her thoughts. "You have enjoyed reading the Bible, Lady Michela?"

Michela was surprised to see one lady had stayed with her. "Yes. It's very comforting," she replied. Looking around the shelves that were within her view, Michela realized that they were not alone. Others browsed in this large multi-chambered library.

"You need comfort?" the lady close to her asked.

"Yes," Michela replied. "My father died… last week."

"Oh, I'm sorry," the lady said. "And Lord Beric and his wife took you in. It must be good to have people to care for you. But I'm surprised you are out so soon… you do not wear mourning dress?"

Michela turned away, feeling deeply embarrassed and at a loss.

"You are… happy… in your new home?" the lady persisted.

"I'm not permitted to speak of it," Michela answered, fearing Beric's wrath.

Elisabet swept into the chamber at that moment. Her eyes flickered fearfully over the pair, standing close together by the window. "What have you been discussing?" Elisabet demanded.

The lady said quickly, "Lady Michela says she is so grief-stricken by her father's passing she cannot discuss anything. She should take a bath and retire early. Tomorrow morning she'll take the King's Test."

"We won't tell Beric that we were apart," Elisabet said, "and we'll make haste to join him or he'll be anxious about our whereabouts."

Soaking in the bath, Michela felt disappointed she had not confided in the lady who had spoken so kindly in the library. Perhaps such a lady would be able to help or advise her? Michela decided that she would never know. Tomorrow was the test. Yes, tomorrow. The sooner it was over, the better, she believed. *And I haven't caused Beric to begin counting; I must not. It'll be my fault if Sarah is whipped! I must keep silent; I mustn't displease Beric.*

Nine

It was the morning of the King's Test.

Elisabet had risen early, and, having requested a copy of the new rules for herself, she sat in the sitting room beneath a bright lamp, reading through the instructions. Being of only a limited literacy, she wished again that June was with them to help her comprehend the wording. But enough was gained from the papers for Elisabet to believe she could use her information both from the rules and from her visit with Alfena to rid her life of Michela forever.

As far as Elisabet was concerned, Michela had to win the King's Test. Even if Alfena had not been able to prophecy certain victory, Elisabet would do all she could to help the girl get it right.

A light breakfast was served just after dawn, causing Beric's ill temper to flare. He always liked to work for two or three hours before indulging in a meal more like a dinner than a breakfast. To have light servings of fruit, cereal and bread was not his choice, certainly not at such an early hour. He was so angry he almost choked. There was no wine to soothe him either, and his animosity seemed to rise by the second. Michela, aware of Beric's simmering tantrum, behaved as though she was invisible, wishing she were.

Then Sir Chezney was announced to their sitting room.

"You've read the rules, Lady Michela?" Chezney asked, looking squarely into Michela's face.

Michela looked at Beric, then at Elisabet.

"We've read the rules for our ward," Elisabet said firmly.

"That's not acceptable. You both know it. Lady Michela must read the rules herself, or have them read to her."

"Read the rules, girl," Beric said, and thrust the sheaf of papers into her hands, "and don't take all day about it!"

Michela's fingers trembled so much, she dropped the sheaf and the papers scattered on the carpet. Two footmen bumped heads in their enthusiasm to gather them up, and Beric uttered a single word, a number.

"One."

Michela, taking the papers into her trembling hands, comprehended the number. It was one stroke for her sister. Already she could see Percival's evil grin, his long unfurled whip. "Please, Lord Beric! No, please..." The papers slipped from her fingers again.

"Two."

With great effort, Michela stood erect while the footmen again collected the papers from off the floor. This time, she held on to them. Taking them to a small table by the window, she set them in their correct numerical order. *I must be quick, and I must concentrate. Two is not life threatening, but if he counts any more, it will be too much to bear. Just think of these rules... then I'll have the test and it'll be over. I'll beg Beric to let me take the strokes.*

With her finger in the center of the page, Michela read through the rules, shuffling the pages as each passed into her memory.

It seemed to both Beric and Elisabet that just seconds had passed when Michela rose and returned the pages to Chezney.

"You've read the rules?" he asked, surprised.

"Yes, Sir Chezney."

"It's impossible," Elisabet said, but a withering look from Beric silenced her. The master believed that Michela had pretended to read the rules to placate him. Such pretence suited Beric. If Michela did not know the rules, he could keep the test turned in his own favor.

"You understand that your guardians may advise you, but you yourself must make the ultimate choices?"

"That's exactly what the rules state," Michela replied, annoyed that he voiced the obvious.

"Good. We shall go to the Gift Chamber then."

~ * ~

Both Beric's and Elisabet's mouths dropped open as their eyes greedily viewed the array of gifts. Since the new rules had been implemented, thus excluding many hopeful but ineligible women, the value of the gifts had been increased. Instead of single pieces, or pairs of jewelry, whole sets were offered. All around the room, footmen opened velvet-lined boxes for Michela to view. Beric and Elisabet stood gaping in desire, their eyes devouring each gift.

Michela, instead of looking at the gifts, watched her guardians. And in turn, Sir Chezney and other attendants stared at Michela in surprise. Usually, the candidate was excited about the beautiful treasures.

"You must examine the gifts, Lady Michela, or how can you make a wise choice, as the rules say?" Chezney urged.

Michela turned to view the chamber as a whole. A footman, over in the corner, opened a door in the wall. To Michela's surprise, a long nose with pointed ears at the top poked itself through the arch-like aperture.

"A horse!" she exclaimed in delight. Moving across to the animal, she carefully stroked his nose, wondering that such a magnificent and valuable animal could be a gift.

"You don't need a horse," Beric's voice hissed into Michela's ear. "Come away from it before I count three."

Chezney noticed that the candidate's joy disappeared as she moved away from the horse. Beric forced her to look at every set of jewelry, then he took her along the line of other gifts. There was a chest of charms containing many items Michela had seen in Neda's chamber, except these were gold-dipped: gold rabbits' feet, golden acorns, a crystal ball on a golden stand, star brooches and earrings with snake-charms engraved into the golden metal, studded with small diamonds.

Lifting a beautiful diamond tiara in trembling hands, Elisabet placed it on Michela's head before returning it to its place. Instead of voicing ridicule that Michela looked like a queen, Elisabet was silent. Michela did look like a queen.

Michela stepped away from Beric and Elisabet as they drew out the objects to view them closer. She moved along the table, looking at other gifts: a spinning wheel with a credit note for one hundred bales of wool, an official land deed for an hundred-acre block of fertile farm-land, a writing desk with quills, ink, paper, everything a secretary needed, a large shelf filled with books, and amongst the titles, a Bible.

Michela saw Beric beckoning.

"This set of jewelry, Michela, and this one; and we will have the chest of gold-dipped charms with its crystal ball," Beric said, indicating the gifts he wanted.

Chezney had seen this performance by Beric before. The rules had been rewritten to deal with such avaricious men.

"Lady Michela must make her own choices," Chezney said.

"She has done so," Beric said firmly, wanting only to take the gifts and leave.

Chezney stepped closer to Michela, saying, "Have you no mind of your own, Lady Michela?"

"My guardian's choices are also mine," Michela said firmly, thinking of Sarah, locked in that cell with the promise of two strokes from Percival's whip hanging over her.

"But you're not considering the need to obey the king's command," Elisabet broke into the conversation. She knew Beric would be furious, but she decided to take the risk. "The rules state you must make the choices you want to make… for the sake of your own future, Michela."

"Now that you've gained your guardians' advice, Lady Michela, and according to the rules, I must ask them both to leave this chamber," Chezney said, and watched as they reluctantly moved out. The door closed.

"Lady Michela, first I must ask you a question. Are you comfortable with your guardians?"

Michela did not answer, but stared at the floor.

"If you're not entirely happy, Lady Michela, I do hope you realize that you may petition the king for a change in your guardianship." Michela's eyes turned to Chezney's as if struck by a wondrous light. "Yes," he said softly, "nothing is impossible. Trust me, child."

Michela could hardly believe her ears. To be freed from Beric? Then, as she thought of Sarah, she bowed her head, thinking of the two strokes she had gained already for her sister.

"What I would like you to do, Michela," Chezney said, having dropped the 'lady,' and stepping even closer, "is to imagine that you are able to begin your life anew, on your own. Which items, of these gifts, would you wish to own then? Would the jewelry be what you want, perhaps as a dowry to attract a worthy husband; or what would you choose? I must insist, Michela, that you keep to the rules and choose from your own heart and not at the whim of your overbearing guardian."

Chezney wanted to say much more. He felt sure that Michela was intimidated in many ways, and he suspected she had a bruise on her cheek and another on her forehead, under the carefully applied cosmetic powder. He chided himself for not having spoken to the ladies who had cared for her; perhaps they would know about the bruises and how she had received them.

Moving around the chamber again, Michela stood by the table upon which sat the land deed. She was not thinking about the gifts, but of Sarah and the possibility that they could be freed from Beric.

"Sir Chezney, Lord Beric is my guardian because of a debt incurred by my father before he died. Is it truly possible that we could be freed from him?"

"We?" he asked.

"I have a little sister," Michela said dully, blinking away threatening tears. "Her name is Sarah; she's only seven years old."

"Anything is possible, Michela. All you have to do is to petition King Alexander for a change in your guardianship."

"How do I do that?" Michela asked.

"You may do it through me, if you wish," Sir Chezney said, hoping fervently that he was not breaking some code of ethics by so offering, then he added, "I'm sure my wife and I could take on your petition if we heard your whole story."

"We... it could be done before we leave here?" Michela asked, scarcely able to conceal her relief and excitement.

"It can be arranged," Chezney said. "My wife's name is Laurissa... she was in the library with you, Michela..."

"Yes, Sir Chezney, I remember her; she was very kind."

"What I wish you to do now, Michela, is to make your choices believing that you will be free to enjoy the gifts yourself; that no one can, or will, take them from you, and that you and your sister will be able to live where you want and with guardians who are compatible."

Michela smiled suddenly, but there were tears in her eyes. With great joy, she said, "I need no other gift than what you have already offered me, Sir Chezney. I thank you from the depths of my heart."

"Then make your choices, Michela, before we cause Lord Beric to have a heart attack from impatience."

Michela laughed lightly at his humor, but stifled the sound as she caught the amused twinkle in the eye of the scribe seated behind the table by the land deed. *How many people here know Beric?* she wondered.

Without further hesitation, Michela said, "In the light of your words and the trust I place in them, Sir Chezney, I choose, in order of preference according to the rules, the shelf of books, the land deed, and the spinning wheel."

"No jewelry?" he asked.

"No, never," she replied.

"Then record Lady Michela's choices," Chezney commanded. In a tone that spoke of disbelief, he asked, "You read and comprehended the rules in that short amount of time?"

"My tutor schooled me to read quickly," Michela said simply. "He was very exact in his training, Sir Chezney. If you wish, I could quote almost word for word what your rules say." Unable to prevent herself, Michela added confidingly, "I'm just hoping and praying that His Majesty will not require me to take the second test."

"Hoping... and praying?" Chezney asked, having gestured for a guard to fetch Michela's guardians.

"Yes," Michela replied, "very fervently, Sir Chezney. I've no desire to meet King Alexander. You must realize that my entering this... this charade... is not my choice, but Beric's."

"Charade?" Chezney asked, surprised. No candidate had ever called the King's Test a charade before. Chezney raised his eyebrows. This beautiful young lady was proving to be very interesting. He found it hard to believe she was for real.

~ * ~

"Michela, dear, tell us what you have chosen..." Elisabet spoke in her honeyed tone, holding her hands out to her ward as if she were the dearest soul on earth to her.

"Yes, Michela, but better still... show us..." Beric said, his eyes on his ward's flushed cheeks. What was it he saw now? Happiness? The light in Michela's eyes alarmed him.

Remembering Sarah, locked in Beric's dungeon, Michela told herself she must remain calm and collected; they were not out of Beric's clutches yet, not at all! She stole a peek at Chezney who nodded at her. His eyes said, 'Trust me,' and Michela felt heartened.

Chezney's eyes are kind and very open... I do feel I can trust him, she thought as she stepped to the bookshelf.

"My first choice was the bookshelf, with the books, of course," Michela said.

"Oh no!" Beric said, shaking his head. "Not books!"

"I'd have liked the writing desk, Lord Beric, but feel perhaps the land deed is more valuable." She stepped past the small roll of paper and said, "The spinning wheel and the wool would be worth many sets of jewelry, Sir Beric, once the wool was spun into hanks. If it were dyed, the wool would treble in value."

"Books, wool, land?" Beric said in despair and anger. "What on earth did you choose those for? What are you saying they're worth?"

"Much more than jewelry, Lord Beric, if you know how to do sums," Michela answered bravely.

"More?" Beric asked, and it dawned on him that she could be right. He swallowed his anger and tried to quiet his mind into concentrating on his ward's claim.

Sir Chezney raised his eyebrows at this revelation. He had not figured this out, either. The test had not been concocted for this purpose, but for ascertaining a young lady's values, her beliefs, and perhaps any wisdom she might have.

"King Alexander has a very busy schedule today, but he shall hear of Lady Michela's choices. Then, if he wishes to have her presented to him, you'll be informed; if not, then the three of you shall be released." Chezney announced. "You may wait in your quarters or perhaps walk in the gardens, provided you inform members of your retinue exactly where you are at all times." His eyes met Elisabet's for a brief second, then the latter looked away.

<h1 style="text-align:center">Ten</h1>

To Elisabet's irritation, Beric was not unhappy with Michela's choices. He ordered her to sit at the table in their private dining room and write down the figures, proving that her choices were more valuable than the sets of precious jewelry, or even the money that could be gained from the sale of the individual gold-dipped charms.

Beric was astounded. Even the books, if sold, were worth a fortune.

Elisabet fumed, pacing the room behind the couple, furious to see Beric so involved with Michela and the figures she was writing on the paper.

"You're sure there were over a hundred books?" he asked in disbelief.

"Yes, Lord Beric. Most of the titles are well sought after, and considering all the books are either new issues, or restored and rebound, they're all very valuable."

"You've done very well for us, Princess," Beric said with a grin on his face.

Elisabet felt relieved when a herald interrupted to give an announcement, "Lady Michela Raynor and her guardians, Lord Beric and Lady Elisabet, will be presented to King Alexander in two hours' time."

Beric's mind had been on nothing else but the calculations Michela had made of the value of the wool once spun and plied into hanks ready for knitting or weaving. Now he had to deal with the fact that they were not returning to Clifton, but were to be presented to the king.

"I have nothing to wear," lamented Elisabet. They still wore the clothes they had intended to wear home last night.

The lady Michela now recognized as Chezney's wife, Laurissa, stepped forward, saying, "We've a large wardrobe here at the palace, Lady Elisabet; if you and your ward would like to come and choose..."

"I'll go. Michela will wait here." Elisabet said, not wanting Michela to choose a black dress, but something much more attractive.

"I want a bath," Beric ordered. In a matter of minutes, a bathtub was carried through the doors of the sitting room, through his wife's bedchamber and into his own, and the water began to arrive for it, vessel by vessel. Beric removed his jacket and set it on the couch. His attention flew back to Michela's figures.

"Write down the extensions for the wool, once dyed. Don't bother calculating the cost of labor; I'll use my slaves."

Having exhausted the extent of the revenue from all three gifts—the land planted with imaginary grain, and producing a bumper crop—Beric whistled as he strode through the sitting room, through his wife's bedchamber and to his own. The land would go on producing for years... he had visions of chests filled with gold pieces.

Michela had never heard Beric whistle before, and she laughed. Two footmen in the room raised their eyebrows to hear the rare sound of this lady's laughter. Before they could blink, Michela snatched up Beric's jacket and disappeared into her own bedchamber, taking the garment with her.

As fast as her slim fingers allowed, Michela removed the two weapons. Her amazing memory helped her as she opened the barrels and removed the bullets. Fixing their safety catches again, she replaced the pistols in their respective pockets and returned the garment to its place on the couch, arranging it exactly as she remembered. The next instant, Elisabet entered, commanding that Michela go with her.

"We may bathe in an exquisite bathroom adjacent to the ladies' dressing room and wardrobe, Michela. One room is walled with mirrors. Such a wardrobe—wardrobes, I should say. Such vibrant colors. There are no gowns dismal enough to remind one of funerals. You may choose something for yourself. I've enough to do to look for my own gown. Imagine! We're to be presented to the king!"

Bathed, dried and dressed in an amazingly short amount of time, Elisabet continued to lament that she had not brought her own hairdresser and make-up artist. Her regrets soon vanished when Laurissa arrived with employees of the court to take care of these matters.

Elisabet, her own hair done in a style more elegant than ever before, watched and issued commands on the styling of Michela's hair, and on her make-up.

"Cover the mark on her cheek, and fashion her hair forward to hide the one at her hairline."

~ * ~

Twelve minutes before the hour, all three were ready. After walking to the corridor outside the throne room, they had only four minutes to wait.

The bookcase and books, the spinning wheel, and the land deed, were all carried into the throne room ahead of Michela and her guardians. Never before had the books and shelf been chosen, nor the wheel. As Michela and her guardians were announced, King Alexander's court converged into the great chamber, following the first candidate to be presented to their king since the issuing of the new rules for the King's Test.

Sir Chezney himself made the announcement: "Lord Beric, Lady Elisabet, and Lady Michela Elizabeth Alexandria Raynor, of Clifton Province."

Chezney had not been able to gain an audience with the king before this presentation, because King Alexander's schedule had been too tight. It had, in fact, been very difficult to fit this encounter into the king's itinerary today. Because Chezney was afraid Beric would refuse to wait until tomorrow, he had insisted that the trio be presented today.

As Chezney watched Michela curtsying, he was washed with the sensation that she had spoken truly; she had no wish to meet King Alexander.

The king did not glance at Michela; his attention was upon the small list of her choices, then his eyes alighted on the bookshelf, now filling with the books, carried in small piles by attendants. Closing his eyes, the king leaned his head on the back of his throne, as was his habit when bored. To switch his attention suddenly from interesting matters of state to a young woman and her desire to wed him was irksome.

When the chosen gifts were arranged, King Alexander opened his eyes. Beric's lumpy over-dressed frame invaded his vision. Having no idea that this was the candidate's guardian, the king felt ill to imagine *this* man wished to be his father-in-law. His eyes moved to Lady Elisabet, and his eyebrows rose—was this the lady— over dressed, over jeweled, and altogether too well done?

Then he saw the young candidate.

Michela did not look at the king, but at the wall to the side of the throne. Her countenance, over-paled with too much powder, did not hide her heart-shaped face, exquisite beyond any the king had seen before. His eyes fell back on Elisabet and he could not believe this woman was the young lady's mother. Nor did Beric seem old enough to be her father. They looked like ill-chosen, unmatched actors in a melodrama.

"Read the names of our guests again," the king commanded, realizing he had not listened. *It's inexcusable*, he admonished himself. He said, "The relationship of these guests was not given, and we wish to know."

"Lord Beric, Lady Elisabet, and their ward, Lady Michela Elizabeth Alexandria Raynor, all from Clifton, Your Majesty," Chezney announced.

The king stared at the list of gifts: and then, he said aloud, "The books, the land deed, and the spinning wheel." This was the first time no jewelry had been chosen, and no chest of charms. King Alexander looked again at Michela and saw that she was very slim and lovely, especially so compared to the ugly man at her side. She looked as though she did not belong; she was somehow separate from all that was happening around her. The king wondered, cynically, if she were trying to remember her lines.

"Tell us, Lady Michela," the king asked, "why have you chosen these particular gifts?"

Beric opened his mouth to explain the wonderful perception and intelligence of his ward, but remembered that Chezney had warned him not to speak unless specifically asked to do so by the king. He closed his mouth and turned to Michela.

"The gifts I chose, Your Majesty, are the most valuable of the gifts," Michela replied.

"Most valuable?" he asked, wishing she would look at him.

"Yes, Your Majesty."

"In terms of monetary value?" he asked, having discerned a double meaning in her words.

"Yes, Your Majesty, in monetary value as well."

"Which then, of the books, is your favorite?" He waited, and as she did not reply, he said, "Come now, you've chosen the books and must have a knowledge of the titles... or is it that you do not know them, and wish to gain more knowledge?"

Attracted by the deep tones in his voice, but feeling threatened by his questioning, Michela looked at King Alexander for the first time. She had expected to see someone as old as Beric, or older, and felt entirely unprepared for the magnificence and attraction of the young king who sat on the imperial throne of Rompavia. His grandeur took her breath away. Then, remembering Beric's evil dominance, she wondered if she could trust this king, and then she chastened herself for feeling so awestruck. Her heart pounded in her breast; he was so magnificent! She had to remind herself, *This king has power over Beric. I don't know him. Looks can be deceiving. Perhaps I should despise him... Sarah and I could even be worse off if we're at this king's mercy... he who designed this test to gain a queenly wife who can spin gold from straw. How can he be so deluded?*

Michela's eyes darted to the crimson velvet gracing the wall behind the throne. She swallowed, believing and hoping that her reply would put him off her forever. "The Bible is my favorite, Your Majesty. I revere the Bible with all my heart. It's the most valuable possession I could own. It... the book has value within its pages that cannot be calculated in fiscal terms..." Remembering Beric's command that she lower her eyes in his own presence, Michela suddenly felt frightened; it was the king of Rompavia she addressed. He had twice the power, perhaps he dealt twice as violently? It could not be possible, could it? She hated feeling so insecure, so uncertain. Moving her eyes to the floor just in front of her, she waited.

The king sat forward on his throne, his eyes and mind taking in the scene again. He stared at Michela, trying to determine what it was about her that was so different. She was like a statuette, he decided, placed in his throne room contrary to her own wish, not a willing part of this presentation. She seemed to have placed a wide, uncrossable river between herself and all those around her, including her incongruous guardians, and oddly, enough, himself. He finally spoke, "Lord Beric, are you a relative of Lady Michela's?"

Bowing, Beric babbled out the first thing that came to mind; he felt he must grasp this opportunity to defend himself against any association with the Bible. "No, Your Majesty; I'm no relation, but I am Michela's legal guardian. Forgive my ward, for her... her preoccupation with that book! I told her it was of no use other than its resale. She's not been herself since her father died, and she does not take kindly to having a guardian, but we're grateful to you for the gifts, Your Majesty; thank you."

"Who appointed you to be Lady Michela's guardian, Lord Beric?" the king asked.

"The appointment was automatic, Your Majesty. Michela's father, the late Lord Raynor, owed me a great sum of money, Your Majesty." Beric bowed again, knowing he need say no more; a debtor had rights to take over property and guardianship of children if there were no adult heirs to pay back the debts. Until Michela married, the guardian had rights to govern her and her properties.

Turning his eyes to Michela, the king asked, "Move closer, Lady Michela, stand close to the dais step." He waited while she obeyed, then said, "You chose a land deed and a spinning wheel. We should like to know the specific reasons for these choices, Lady Michela."

Taking a deep breath, Michela wished she could be anywhere but here in this throne room. How could she have made such a mistake as to choose the spinning wheel? The king wanted a wife who could spin, did he not? She swallowed again, feeling intimidated. *He's interested in me because of the spinning wheel,* she told herself.

Looking up into the king's intense brown eyes was too much to bear, so Michela dropped her gaze again, staring at the step just beneath her.

"Perhaps, Your Majesty, I may find myself with enough time on my hands to be able to spin. I can spin fleece to yarn, and I have the skill needed to knit it. And the land... I have a younger sister... I would like to imagine that we could earn a living off the land as well. One never knows when one might be alone in the world. My father's death was very unexpected. I... I chose the spinning wheel with the wool, and the land, entirely for their earning capacities."

The king stared at Michela, wishing she would look up at him; how could he read her character if he could not see her eyes? But she did not oblige and King Alexander searched the large chamber for a glimpse of Chezney. Then their eyes met, and to the king's surprise, Chezney gave a nod.

"Lady Michela, it pleases me to announce that you qualify for the second test," King Alexander said, adding, "It will be taken tonight." He frowned then, because he saw that the object of his royal favor was not pleased about his announcement. She did not smile; she did not giggle, as others had, neither did she curtsy and thank him as expected, and appropriate. As the king stared at her, she stiffened, and he had the unnerving sensation that Michela was not only disagreeable but she was not acting at all. He knew he must learn more about this candidate.

In the deep silence, Michela stiffened even more, and her eyes moved up to view the throne; the king's elaborate robes, his face, and his jeweled crown. She would have to endure a second test. There seemed no way out. Then she felt Beric's horrible presence at her side.

Beric was amazed to hear the king's announcement. The acceptance of his ward and her choices was incomprehensible to this conceited man. He waited for Michela to voice her appreciation to the king, and when she was silent, he whined out a volley of gratitude for the great honor bestowed upon him and his wife.

Michela bowed her head, unable to look into the king's searching brown eyes.

"What does Lady Michela have to say?" the king demanded at last.

Looking back to lock her eyes with his as in battle, Michela answered in her soft voice, "I'd rather not take the second test, Your Majesty."

"You'd rather... not... take the test?" King Alexander repeated in astonishment. Ripples of amazement and speculation ran through the court. The king looked from Beric's thunderous face, to Michela's pale determined countenance, then at Chezney's smile. Staring back at Michela, he noted that her blue-green eyes were very earnest and open. "Why not, Lady Michela?" he asked.

"It is voiced... that... I must spin straw into gold," Michela said. She waited for him to deny it, but he gave nothing away. His face seemed to her as expressionless as granite. "If that is what's expected, Your Majesty, then I must tell you that it's a waste of time; I can't do it." Again she locked her eyes with his, and again she gained no answer in the brown depths of his tenacious stare. As if she needed to explain her heart to him, she added, "It's not my wish that I'm here, Your Majesty, but my guardian's." In these few words she told the king of Rompavia that she had no desire to marry him. Murmurs in the court grew louder. Michela blushed and looked away, unaware of Beric's fists clenching and unclenching at her side.

King Alexander smiled faintly. Never before had anyone admitted they knew about the test before they took it. Not one maiden had been unwilling before, either. Most, indeed, were over-eager. It had been sickening, as sickening as Beric's obvious urge to strike his ward right now! He turned his royal stare upon the candidate's guardian. Beric bowed, unclenching his fists.

The king changed his smile to a frown. He thought for a few minutes.

With a wave of his royal hand to gain silence, King Alexander stood. He stepped down from the dais, and Michela curtsied low, while Beric bowed again.

"Rise," he commanded, standing close to Michela. "Look at your king," he commanded when she left her focus on the floor.

Michela lifted her eyes, moving them up the royal figure in front of her, from the ermine of his cloak that graced the marble floor, up to the royal medallions around his broad chest, up, up. She blushed as her stare fixed with the king's. He was so close, and she could see the corner of his lip twitch slightly. While she struggled to catch her breath, his eyes circled her face and lingered on her hair.

"You will take the second and most important part of the King's Test, Lady Michela. We wish you to try... tonight," he said softly. Then the king of Rompavia strode from the throne room amidst sweeping obeisance.

Eleven

Escorted back to the guest apartment, Michela sensed the anger bound up in the wide frame of her guardian. Then, remembering King Alexander standing so close to her, she shivered, not from cold, but from remembrance of his handsome face: the cynical set of his lips, the slight quiver, the way his eyes had seemed to pierce her soul. Knowing she was attracted to him, and blaming him for his magnificence and striking good looks, she wondered if his palace were not a more threatening place to be than Beric's castle. Beric's behavior matched his appearance, but this king—who held sway over the kingdom—he was like a book with a beautifully embellished cover. Who was to know what its pages would reveal? Feeling emotionally drained, she was then unable to think of anything else but those dark brown eyes and the King of Rompavia.

Discounting him utterly and discrediting the foreign feeling of fascination she could not foil she allowed her mind to disparage him.

King Alexander wishes me to try... he said... he wants me to spin straw into gold! How can he look so intelligent, yet expect such a thing of me? How can our king expect magic to be performed? He's likely to be worse than Beric... at least my guardian does not expect me to turn straw into gold.

I don't understand him... his eyes... he's arrogant and proud... he wants everything his own way... 'we wish you to try... tonight,' he said. He sounded sincere, but he's impossible!

When they arrived back in the sitting room of the apartment, Beric was so angry he almost exploded! There were few words in his vocabulary, other than curse words to vent his deep rage. At first, he could not speak, then he stuttered, striving unsuccessfully to find socially acceptable words to vocalize his aggravation.

"You... you... you dimwitted fool nincompoop, numbskull... I... I... you... how could you? Of all the..." taking a deep breath and ignoring their retinue, Beric erupted into a barrage of oaths and curses, making everyone in the room gasp in shock and shame.

Servants bearing trays of refreshments entered the room, and Beric's verbal ferocity fell into recess.

"Tea, Lady Michela? Lady Elisabet?" a waiter asked. "Tea, Lord Beric?"

"Yes, please," Michela replied, grateful for the diversion. How she hated herself for casting off Beric's language so effortlessly this time. It was as though she had grown a hard, thick protective shell under which to weather the storm and thunder without feeling the assault.

"Bring a decanter of wine, for both my husband and me," Elisabet demanded.

Beric began to eat and drink, and his anger subsided a little with each large mouthful he consumed. When the edge had vanished off his endless appetite, and he had consumed copious amounts of wine, Beric prepared himself to tell his ward just how displeased he was with her. Not only would Percival whip her sister, but also he would have her whipped when they arrived home. Ungrateful wench! However, before Beric could speak, Chezney entered the chamber.

"I've good news for you, Lord Beric, Lady Elisabet, Lady Michela," the king's adviser said enthusiastically. "King Alexander has requested that you dine with him this evening before the test."

Michela stood when Sir Chezney entered the room. Now she prepared herself to refuse this unexpected invitation; 'request', he called it. She did not want to dine with the king, nor take the test. How could she bear to be near the king, His Majesty, one moment longer than necessary? Her emotions regarding him confused her, and although she wanted to discount him as a fool, she found her inner being longing to see him again. She quivered at the thought of being near to him, not from fear, but from anticipation. *My feelings are all askew,* she mused, *I am double-dealing with myself...*

"Thank you, Sir Chezney, and of course we accept, with thanks for the honor," Beric gushed. He looked sideways at his ward, and said, "What a privilege to dine with His Majesty; say thank you, Michela!"

Inclining her head slightly, Michela curtsied. She almost bit her tongue, drawing back a caustic retort. She wondered how she could trust Chezney? All he had done was make matters worse.

"I shall return at six, then," Chezney said. He left the room, beaming about the matter. The king had never requested that any one of the candidates dine with him before; that would have appeared untimely, and people would gossip. However, King Alexander had commanded that the three be invited, and Chezney knew his king was greatly intrigued and challenged by this young maiden who, unlike any other, did, indeed, have an opinion and a mind of her own! He, himself, could not wait to have private time with the king to tell him all he had discovered. And, with his wife's help, Chezney determined to find out Michela's whole story.

"Six? How can they dine so early?" Beric said, his mind in a whirl. It was such a privilege! To dine with King Alexander!

"What shall I wear?" Elisabet cried, thinking of the time it would take to choose an evening gown from the massive selection in the palace wardrobes. "Come, Michela, we must make ourselves look stunning!"

~ * ~

The palace dining hall was an amazing size, but Michela heard someone telling her guardians that it was not as large or as impressive as the banqueting hall. As in Clifton, the court and guests were announced first, but instead of standing at their designated table places, they stood in a reception line to await the entry of the king.

Michela half expected King Alexander to pause as he passed her. He spoke to one or two as he moved along the line. She remained in her lowest position of obeisance, and kept her eyes on the floor. When he did not stop, she could not prevent a feeling of disappointment flooding her veins. She wondered again why her emotions were proving to be such traitors.

The king sat at the head of the one table. Chezney escorted Michela to a place—about a third of the way along the table—on the king's right. Elisabet and Beric sat to Michela's left, Laurissa on her right with Chezney beside his wife. Other advisers and guests sat in their elected places.

Michela's calculating mind quickly did a tally: over eighty places had been set at the one table; she could hardly see the other end. If the places had been arranged closer together, over a hundred could sit at this incredible table. Then, as the places filled, Michela realized that the opposite end of the table to the king remained vacant. She blushed, knowing this important seat had once been occupied by the king's mother, and was reserved for the future queen.

Beric reached for food and would have started eating, only a sacred hush stopped him, as well as a gentle dig from the elbow of his wife. A priestly-garbed man stepped to the king's side and offered a prayer of thanksgiving to God for the day, the king's health and the food. Michela bowed her head with pleasure. She repeated the prayer in her mind, and was slow to look up after the 'amen'. To find the king's eyes upon her face made her blush. She hoped he disliked her, but knew in that instant that his look was not of dislike. Michela felt more dislike for him surge up inside her. How she longed to be in Rayburn Castle and to have everything as it was when her father was alive.

The meal seemed long and drawn out to Michela; then, as she thought of the test, she changed her mind and wished it would go on forever! To save herself from looking at the king, Michela cast her attention in the other direction, feeling miffed that she had to look at her guardians.

Beric devoured amazing amounts of food. As Michela looked past Elisabet, she saw her guardian commanding the footman to pile up his plate again. Michela felt sure Beric did not chew, but just pushed the food into his mouth and swallowed. He ignored the utensils supplied at his place, but both Elisabet and Michela used theirs with expertise.

After the fourth course, the ladies moved to another chamber as was the custom of the day. Michela found herself the center of attention; they remarked on the pretty gown she had chosen, asking if the color, pale mauve, was worn because she was in mourning.

Answering their questions as abruptly as she could without appearing offensive, Michela felt overwhelmed by the ladies' friendliness, their lack of hostility. Elisabet gained attention by extolling Michela's amazing abilities as a clerk and secretary. She found she was both admired and envied, to be guardian of such beauty and intelligence.

Michela realized what was happening; Elisabet was being separated from her. It was deliberate. About twenty-five women were in the room, almost all between her and her guardian's wife.

"Lady Michela... come this way." Laurissa spoke urgently, and with another woman, Michela found herself seated in an alcove, behind a concealing curtain at the end of the salon.

"Quickly... you must tell us everything, Lady Michela," Laurissa said, then introduced her companion, "This is Janice, Sir Tippet's wife. Tippet and Chezney, our husbands, are King Alexander's closest counselors." She paused. As if to gain both Michela's trust and to encourage her to talk she said, "You must trust us, Michela. Chezney told us that you have been a victim of injustice. Is it true that your father, Lord Raynor, owed Lord Beric much money?"

"Lord Beric says he did," Michela replied. "I kept Father's books and had no record of the debt. But Sir Beric had documents…"

Michela wondered if she could truly trust these women.

How can I read their true character? I cannot… I can only trust their words… I have no other choice.

Tears pricked her eyes, and she felt a warm hand squeeze hers.

"Trust us, Michela. We truly wish to help you," Janice urged.

Michela sensed a genuine tone in Janice's voice. She decided to forget King Alexander and the test; she must concentrate on the offered friendship of these two women. *What do I have to lose?* she asked herself. *What, really can be worse than Sarah in a dungeon, awaiting a whipping from Percival at Beric's command? I must try to help her… perhaps these women have hearts…*

Michela drew a deep breath. Keeping her story to a minimum and depreciating the pain, she told of her father's unexpected death and Beric's subsequent takeover of Rayburn Castle, his annexing of the province. The women did not speak until Michela had finished, having told them that coming to the capital was not her idea nor her desire.

"Where's your sister, Sarah, now?" Janice asked.

"She's a prisoner in Sir Beric's castle… in a cell, in the… the torture chamber. I… I only agreed to come here to Avingworth because Lord Beric threatened he would whip Sarah if I refused. He has already stated that he plans to have her whipped when we return…"

"Let me be sure we have this right," Janice said, with amazement in her voice, "your sister Sarah's life is being threatened to make you do Beric's bidding?"

"Yes, that's Beric's way," Michela admitted. "I would not have come if Beric had not threatened Sarah the way he did."

"You really don't want to take the test tonight?" Laurissa asked.

"No," she replied. Shaking her head, she smiled pensively and said, "It'll be a waste of time. It's difficult for me to imagine that our king…

wants me to take part in acting out a fairy tale. King Alexander said he wishes me to try, but I cannot even do that, because I believe it to be impossible."

Both ladies smiled. The King's Test had been gossiped about, but the truth never discovered. King Alexander wanted someone just like Michela who did not believe the fairy tale and would speak the truth.

"You may find everything to be very different from what you imagine, Michela," Laurissa said. "Our advice, Michela, is that you never come to a conclusion before you have all the facts."

Michela nodded, believing with all her heart that she could trust Laurissa and Janice. She said sweetly, "There's a proverb that says that, Laurissa. I must keep remembering it; thank you." Then her face grew serious as she continued, "It's not just for myself that I fear, Laurissa and Janice, but for Sarah, my sister. Beric is... he is violent beyond anyone I have ever known or could have imagined..." The tinkling of a crystal bell interrupted the conversation, and Michela knew that her time with these ladies was over.

"We'll see what we can do," Laurissa said. "You must go for the test, now, Michela. Shall we wish you good luck?"

Grimacing, Michela answered, "I don't believe in 'luck', but if you pray to God, please pray for us... especially for Sarah. Have you ever seen a... a dungeon... a torture chamber? My sister is only seven years old..."

Suddenly Laurissa's eyes filled with tears and she could not speak.

Both ladies knew this lovely lady was feeling victimized and tormented. Janice said, "Be assured that we shall not only pray for you, but we shall help bring about some answers to your prayers. Chezney will make sure that King Alexander hears about it all."

~ * ~

It was late... much later than everyone had expected. The chamber to which Beric, Elisabet, and Michela were escorted was a surprise to all three. They had expected a dungeon-like room such as in the Rumplestiltskin story. This room was wood-paneled with bright tapestries and paintings gracing its dark polished walls. The only furniture consisted of two comfortable chairs, a spinning wheel, a stool, and a small wheelbarrow filled with straw.

"Here, put this on," Elisabet said, lifting an amulet from around her neck. "Alfena said that if you put it on in this room it will bring you luck and help you in your task." She held the amulet out for Michela to take.

"I will not wear it," Michela said firmly. The heavy silver had small holes drilled in the back of it, and a musky odor wafted from the piece of jewelry. She took a step backwards.

"Do as Elisabet tells you, Michela," Beric said, stepping nearer his ward.

Elisabet also moved closer, saying, "It's all right Beric. Let her please herself. Alfena said that our ward would be dead within two days if she does not wear this amulet. Perhaps she prefers to be dead. As for me, I do not." So saying, Elisabet lifted the amulet, intending to put it over her own head again.

"Give it here!" Beric demanded, snatching the amulet away. "I need all the luck I can get!" He grinned and added, "Perhaps I'll be able to spin the straw into gold." With fumbling fingers, he put the amulet around his own thick neck and tucked it into concealment. "It doesn't seem such a big task; I thought there'd be a room full of straw, but it's only a little barrow full."

Casting her attention back to Michela, Elisabet asked, "What did you talk about when I was separated from you, Michela? What did you tell those two women who took you aside? You have talked; I can see it on your face!"

"You spoke privately with some women?" Beric asked, alarmed. "What did you tell them?"

"I told them about Father's death. And I said I believed this test to be impossible. It's nonsensical. And no amulet can help anyone spin straw into gold..."

"What else did you talk about, Michela?" Elisabet persisted.

"I asked them to pray… for… us…" She almost said 'for Sarah,' but bit back the name. Reaching down to touch the straw in the wheelbarrow, she shook her head and said, "It's impossible; it's completely impossible."

Beric laughed loudly and unkindly, saying, "Of course it's impossible. That's why Rumplestiltskin has to come. It's just how we handle things later, with the king. He'll want the gold, of course…" Beric strode to the wall and began banging around the panels with his clenched fists. He moved around two walls, and then, on banging the third, he listened to the hollow noise that sounded out from his hammering.

"Here… this is where Rumplestiltskin will enter," he said. Moving to gaze in triumph at his wife, he then sat in an armchair and folded his arms, a smug grin distorting his pudgy face. Elisabet, her face white, positioned herself in the other chair. The prospect of something supernatural happening unnerved her.

Michela, feeling relieved that Beric was not going to command her to wear the amulet or try to spin the straw, sat on the only other seat in the room, the stool.

"All right! The king said you must try, Michela. You know how to spin, girl, so get started." Beric pointed at the wheel. "You go first, then I'll have a go."

Shaking her head, Michela wondered what to say. She could only answer with the truth. "I don't believe in magic… or in Rumplestiltskin."

Standing, Beric stepped close to the chair, his hands on his large hips. "I said you'll try. The king commanded that you try! Will you disobey him, as well as me?

Michela did not answer, but stiffened her back, staring resolutely at the wall.

"You will begin to spin, Michela."

Drawing a breath in frustration, Michela did not look at him.

"Three… four… five… six… seven… eight… nine… ten… Do you realize that your sister will die if she is measured out more than ten?"

Michela suddenly felt anger overcome her fear of Beric and his taunts. Remembering Chezney, she stood and said, "I shall appeal to the king…"

"The king?" Beric asked, and laughed, scoffing, "It's his idea, this test. Do you really think he'll listen to you? The way you just stared in his throne room was enough! Like a dumb-cluck. He must think you're half-witted."

"Please, Lord Beric; I can't spin straw into gold. Whip me if you must whip someone; but please, I implore you, don't whip Sarah." She felt tears slipping down her cheeks.

"Whipping your sister will hurt you far more than…"

"Beric! Look… look!" Elisabet cried, and stood as a wooden panel in the wall slid open. A tiny man stepped through the gap.

"Good evening," the dwarf said, in a high-pitched voice. "I feel sure I can help you."

"Yes… yes, we…"

"I'm addressing the lovely lady. Pray tell me, what's your name?"

Michela stared at the little man in amazement. He looked like an elf, complete with pointed ears and beard, dressed in bright red pixie clothes with a pointed hat, and bells on his little curved pointed shoes. Wiping her tears away with the backs of her fingers, Michela blinked, wondering if he were real.

"Rumplestiltskin!" Elisabet said, sitting down in amazement.

"Her name's Michela," Beric answered, then saying, "You're Rumplestiltskin, and you've come to do the job for us."

"What job?" the dwarf asked, his bright green eyes looking upward into Michela's face.

"Turning the straw into gold," Beric said, impatiently.

"I can only do it at the lady's command," the dwarf said.

"Then do it!" Beric ordered.

"What will you give me?" the dwarf asked, his eyes still on Michela's face.

"She has a land deed…" Reaching into his jacket, Beric pulled it out. Michela stared at him in surprise, wondering how he had gained possession of it. "And she has a spinning wheel… like this one."

"I've plenty of spinning wheels, and I don't need no land."

"Books? Over one hundred books?" Beric offered. At the little dwarf's head shake, he stammered, "A B-b-b-b-bi-bi-ble?"

"You must know what I really want." The dwarf shifted his eyes to look at Beric.

"The first-born child," Beric replied. "If you can make gold from that straw, then you shall have it."

Looking at Michela, the dwarf asked, "You will give me your first-born, Michela?"

"NO! Of course not!" she answered, indignant, then added, "Never!"

"Then I won't do it!" the dwarf said firmly.

Beric was lost for words.

"Who are you?" Michela stepped closer to the dwarf. "You're not Rumplestiltskin! There's no such person, but in a fairy tale." Reaching out her hand, she grasped the creamy-white beard. As she expected, it pulled off in her hands. "It's made of fleece. You're a phony, as I suspected." As the dwarf stepped backwards, Michela scolded him as she would a naughty child. "You ought to be ashamed of yourself, whoever you are. And you may tell your master the same. Tell him… tell him, I will have nothing to do with this… this… charade!"

Continuing his swift little steps backwards, the dwarf disappeared through the wall. With a click, the wall closed. He was gone, and the place bore no sign of the opening.

Beric hurried to the wall and banged on it with both fists. "Come back! Come back! Come back!" he shouted. Wheeling around, he advanced on Michela with his fists still clenched. "Now see what you've done, you idiotic shrew! That was your chance! I could… I will…" He belched out a string of expletives, then raised his fist, and Michela backed away from him.

Clickety-click…

Beric wheeled around at the sound, his fist still raised.

"I'm back... I'm back... Who's getting upset? What do you have for me, young man, if I turn the straw into gold?"

"Let me think..." Beric replied, dropping his fist into his other hand, unable to believe his good luck. His stance changed to that of compliance. "What do you want?" he asked, forgetting that the dwarf had already told him.

"A slave... all I have ever wanted is a slave..." the dwarf said nervously, quickly.

"I'll give you one," Beric promised, "and if you come back to Clifton with me, I'll give you a slave every time you turn straw into gold."

"I'd be most satisfied with one slave."

"You may have one then. She's not much older than a baby... and compliant, and rather pretty..." Beric turned to view Michela's reaction to his offer.

"No!" she cried. "You can't do that! You'll not offer my sister as a slave!" She saw the gleam in Beric's eye and said quietly, "Give me away as a slave, Lord Beric, but not Sarah."

"We'll have to see if he can do it," Beric said. "Spin the straw into gold, then, Rumpelstiltskin, and you shall have not one, but two slaves. You can have two."

"I've done it already," the dwarf replied. "It saves time. Wait here and I'll be back in two shakes of a dog's tail."

With that, the little man stepped backwards through the door. Beric stooped to look, but it was very low and dark.

In the silence, Michela heard whispering coming from the cavity. She wondered who was on the other side; how much had they heard? Was that the king's voice? What was this performance? Was it a test... or what? The whispers further confirmed that the dwarf was not acting on his own, but Michela's ears told her that the king was there. He had been listening. He was giving instructions to the dwarf. Wringing her hands together, Michela had the same sensation that had swamped her when Beric took over her father's castle; it was all a bad dream.

She looked at Elisabet, sitting on the edge of her seat, engrossed, as if she believed all of this was real.

Beric crouched down, peering into the dark aperture. He moved closer, then pulled away, standing up. The dwarf returned, wheeling in front of him a barrow filled with gold.

"Here it is, and I shall accept two slaves!" the dwarf said. "You may have the gold, sir, if you promise me two slaves from your own household."

"Yes, yes, that's what I said," Beric agreed as he knelt and buried his hands in the threads of pure gold.

"Say it then: you'll give me two slaves of my choice, from your own household."

"I'll give you any two slaves you choose, from my own household," Beric parroted, "and I can have all this?" He snickered loudly and turned to Michela, saying, "If you don't answer the king rightly when he comes, you'll find yourself given away, Michela."

"I'll be back," the little man said as he lifted the handles of the barrow filled with straw, and disappeared.

Elisabet joined her husband, cooing over the gold. Beric sat on the floor beside the barrow, seeking to weigh it, piece by piece, in his hands. Biting on a thicker strand of the shining metal, he said, "It's gold, it's real gold!"

Michela moved across to the armchairs and sank into one. Her mind raced about the dwarf and his act; she wanted to comprehend it, but found it had no meaning to her. When Elisabet joined her, Michela stood. Pacing to the door, Michela wondered when the king would come and what she would say to him.

The main door opened, and Michela gained a glimpse of the distinctive little dwarf standing outside the door.

King Alexander himself strode into the room, followed by Chezney and another man.

"My name is Tippet, Lady Michela." The third man smiled, and bowed.

"I saw you... at dinner, and I met your wife, Janice," Michela said.

"And you succeeded," Tippet said, his eyes upon the gold.

"No," Michela said earnestly, "that gold was not spun from the straw. It was brought in here by..."

"Shut up!" Beric said rudely, having stood to bow. Then he shrugged, and countermanded, "Tell them what happened."

"A dwarf brought it in," Michela said firmly. "He was outside the door when you entered, Your Majesty. You must have seen him... you had been speaking with him..."

"Invite him in, Sir Tippet," the king commanded. Turning back to Michela, he smiled and asked, "And what did you offer this dwarf?"

"It was my deal, Your Majesty. The gold for a couple of slaves, chosen from my household," Beric answered. "Any person who can change straw into gold should have what he wants."

The dwarf entered the room, and the king spoke, saying, "This is my little friend, John. Tell Lord Beric here which two slaves you would like, John." The king's eyes were brimming with laughter, and Michela did not miss this fact. But the twinkles only served to confuse her.

John, the little man, pointed at Beric, saying, "You offered me two slaves of my choice from your household, didn't you?"

"Yes, my friend," Beric answered.

"Then I shall choose you, Beric, and your wife! I want you both." John said, smiling broadly. "Your greed has been your pitfall! You shall be my slave, Beric."

Beric's smile dropped from his face like an over-ripe apple from a shaken tree. His eyes darted about for a way of escape... then they grew glazed as he backed away from the king.

"NO!" Elisabet screamed, her eyes on Michela. "You conniving, scheming, manipulative little cheat!"

Beric's brow speckled with perspiration. Stepping closer to John, he said, "You tricked us, you devious little devil!" He turned on his wife, shouting, "We came to the capital just to have everything go against us like this!" Stepping closer to John, he continued, "How dare you claim that I, Lord Beric, of Clifton Castle, shall be YOUR slave!"

He swiveled to glare at Michela. He yelled, "This...this...disaster... it's all YOUR fault!"

Michela drew a sharp breath as she saw Beric's eyes flicker and narrow. Remembering his past reactions, instinct told her that Beric's reaction would be to force his way from this situation with some act of violence. Beric was boxed in, like a cornered predator. That he was in the presence of the King of Rompavia would likely have escaped his addled mind. Michela opened her mouth to scream a warning but Elisabet cried Beric's name first, and ran to him, flinging herself behind his back as if diving for protection. In the same instant, Beric drew a pistol from inside his jacket, pointing it directly at Michela's head. At this close range, a bullet would kill her.

"Come here, Michela! No one makes a fool of me, not twice!" His voice was hoarse, and with a flick of his finger, he released the safety catch, now turning the pistol to point at the king who took a step closer in concern for Michela.

For one brief millisecond, the king's eyes met with Michela's and it seemed to both that the whole world stood still. It was as though their two hearts were one.

Beric's voice shattered the fusion. "Not a step more, or you're dead!"

Twelve

Beric's voice barked out again, "Come here, Michela!"
Everyone saw, with dismay, that, though Beric's face was distorted and purpled with rage, his hand behind the pointed pistol was rock steady.

John, the timid little dwarf, pressed his hands over his ears, waiting in shock for the big bang.

"Put the pistol down, Beric!" Chezney cried in alarm. They had never thought to search the men who escorted the maidens when they came for the King's Test. This was a cordial social event. Such a situation as this was unprecedented. Their king could get injured, or worse, killed! Chezney had never felt so afraid for the king whom he loved like a son.

Michela stepped resolutely between the pistol point and King Alexander. Everyone in the small chamber knew that she was in control of herself and they saw her deliberately sidestep to block the path of a bullet if fired at the king.

Imagining that King Alexander might step forward and move Michela aside to challenge Beric, Chezney firmly grasped the king's left arm while Tippet took his right. They were not going to allow their king to interfere in this life-threatening confrontation.

"We're leaving here," Beric announced. "You'll come with me, Michela. Everyone will stand aside! Elisabet, keep close to me…" Beric desperately wanted to return to the safety and security of his castle. He felt sure that, once he was back in Clifton, he could block out this freedom-threatening episode.

"No!" Michela spoke firmly, taking a small step backwards. "I'll not come with you, Lord Beric. Shoot me if you must. I'd prefer that to spending another day in your castle." Tilting her chin, and reminding herself that she had removed the bullets from the pistols, she sought to coerce him into surrendering. "Can't you see that you cannot escape from here, Lord Beric? You should do as Sir Chezney suggests and put the pistol down. It would be better for everyone, especially for you, Lord Beric."

"You… you…" Beric could not speak for rage; neither could he think straight. Aiming for Michela's forehead, he squeezed the trigger.

A dull click sounded out, as ominous as the discharge of a bullet because the latter was expected. Beric squeezed the trigger again and another click interrupted the somber hush of the room. With a step forward, Beric's eyes searched Michela's. "You unloaded it!" he screamed, pulling the second pistol from the other side of his jacket.

"Guards! Guards! Guards!" A chorus of men's voices rose from the chamber.

Little John's high-pitched voice joined the cry, as he screamed, "Guards! Hurry! Help! Guards!"

Two guards flung open the doors and advanced, followed by two more. Beric attempted to discharge the second firearm. Had it been loaded, Michela would have been shot through her heart.

A trio of dull clicks told the tale. The second pistol was empty. In great fury, the thwarted murderer threw the pistols at Michela. With a deft flick of her head, she avoided the first, but the second, the heavier, struck her on her temple. In the same instant, she saw the naked blade of a dagger as Beric pulled the weapon from a concealed sheath on his belt.

Michela sighed and closed her eyes. It felt like arms of irresistible sleep reached out and snatched her into blissful darkness and void. She had no idea, as she sank to the floor, that she had been knocked unconscious.

Confusion reigned. While four guards grappled with Beric to immobilize him and take the dagger away without being stabbed, Tippet hurried to join them. It was five against one, and Beric howled, roared, and fought like a rabid bear.

One guard received a gash to his arm, and Tippet was bitten twice. Finally, the guards secured Beric, face down, to the floor, but still he struggled and bucked his body, swearing out the vilest verbiage in vicious frenzy. One guard, sitting on Beric's back, twisted around so that he could ease his knee across the back of Beric's neck. Leaning with all his might, he pressed until Beric's verbal explosion ceased and the man was silent.

Elisabet, her hands covering her face, backed into a corner, petrified into passivity. Her eyes were upon Michela's face and Elisabet believed her ward was dead, just as Alfena had prophesied.

King Alexander's attention was also upon Michela, and he knelt beside her. The ugly bruise on her temple seemed to darken even as he stared at it. A teardrop of blood trickled from a tiny tear in the skin near the corner of her eye. Her face was white and her eyes closed. He wondered if she were even breathing.

Chezney also knelt, leaning over Michela, concerned. "Send for a doctor!" he called.

More guards dashed into the chamber, and Beric was hauled to his feet. Sullen and subdued, he stared at the still form on the floor.

In a fit of satisfaction, he grinned. To all appearances, Michela looked as one who was dead.

"Take him away before that smirk falls from his shoulders!" the king said. He felt so angry with Beric, he could have killed him there and then himself! He looked at Elisabet and commanded, "Take them both out of my sight!"

Gently gathering Michela into his strong arms, the king issued commands. "Fetch your wives, Chezney, Tippet; and tell the doctor to come to the first guest chamber. We must do everything we can to make Lady Michela comfortable."

Within moments the palace was ablaze with the terrible news that an assassination attempt had been made on the king, but was foiled by a beautiful young maiden who shielded King Alexander by stepping between a madman's pistol and their beloved king.

It was not long before the news passed from mouth to ear, on and on across the city of Avingworth. The story grew more dramatic every time it was told.

Very soon a crowd gathered at the palace gates; the people wanted to see for themselves that their king was still alive.

Only when King Alexander, his face lit by large torches held by guards, appeared on a palace balcony, did the people believe he was safe and well. A loud cheer sounded out as subjects saluted their king.

After this, all attention was upon the young maiden—reported to be unconscious and near death.

~ * ~

Michela opened her eyes to find herself lying on a large four-poster bed. Janice had untied the sash around Michela's small waist, seeking to make her more comfortable. Michela had been there only minutes, but time had no meaning, and she imagined herself to be somewhere in the past.

Laurissa drew a rug up over Michela's dress. Michela's hands felt ice cold.

Like everyone who awakes in an unfamiliar place, Michela asked, "Where am I? What happened?"

"You've a nasty bump on your head and the doctor is coming. Just lie still, dear; he'll be here in a minute," Janice answered softly.

"Is this Beric's castle?" Michela asked, feeling confused. She closed her eyes, asking, "Where is Father?" Remembrance of her sister, Sarah, and the dungeon cell made her eyes open in dread. "Sarah... Sarah... no. Don't let him hurt Sarah."

"You're in Avingworth, Michela, in King Alexander's palace," Laurissa said. "Your sister, Sarah, is coming to be with you..."

Michela's eyes closed and she moaned softly. Then to both Janice and Laurissa, she seemed to cease breathing.

Janice leaned her ear gently on Michela's chest, listening and releasing a sigh of relief to hear the sound of a heartbeat.

After the doctor had examined Michela, he told the dismayed king, "She should be left undisturbed so that she can go in peace... her end is near. She will slip into a coma very soon. Time will reveal the truth of my prognosis... I'm sorry, Sire, but it will all be over within forty-eight hours."

The next time Michela awoke, she heard the doctor's soft but deep voice. He was asking questions of Tippet and his wife about the episode with Beric. To the confused girl, the doctor's deep fatherly voice sounded like her own father's.

"Father?" she called, trying to sit. The room was dim; there was just one lone candle burning, and Michela felt drained. Her temple and eyes throbbed as if her heart were beating in them. She fell back against the soft pillow.

"I'm here," the doctor said, taking her hand.

Sighing, Michela closed her eyes. The doctor gently pried her fingers from his. Standing up, he saw that King Alexander had entered the guest room. The doctor bowed. It was now after midnight.

"Father... don't leave me!" Michela cried in a broken voice. She tried to focus on the figures near her bed. "Father... I can't see you... it's dark and cloudy... Father..."

King Alexander pulled a chair to the bedside and took Michela's hand in his. He increased the pressure on the small hand, longing to be able to impart life and warmth to its frigid feel. Due to the intense pain he felt deep inside, his eyes filled with tears.

"Warm the room; light the fire; bring some bed-bricks. Lady Michela's hand feels like ice," the king commanded, wondering why this had not been done already. He took both hands into his own, rubbing them, willing life into them, not missing the doctor's shaken head and look of hopelessness.

Michela felt comforted by the pressure of the warm hands on hers. She wanted to wake up and talk, but something prevented her. She felt tired, so tired. Words trembled on her lips then disappeared as if blown away by an intangible wind.

"Sarah... where is Sarah?" she asked again.

"Sarah is coming," the king replied, "She'll be here soon." He saw her eyes open and wondered if Michela comprehended his words. "We've sent... an escort... to rescue Sarah and to bring her here... to you."

The feel of warmth in her hands, being massaged by such a loving touch, and the words of assurance soothed Michela and calmed her agitation. She felt safe. She felt she could believe the words of the king. He would keep his word. Closing her eyes, she succumbed to the void that wanted to envelop her and fell into a deep sleep.

The king sat staring at the still face, watching the rug rising and falling evenly with her breathing. He could see a faint pulse at her neck moving with each heartbeat. Michela's hands felt warmer and he kissed them, knowing he had hopelessly lost his heart to this brave young maiden. When she died, he knew his heart would break.

Thirteen

The king's army arrived in Clifton an hour after midnight. The captain organized his men-at-arms into companies to surround the castle, planning an attack if entry could not be gained through the gates.

Faced with a declaration that the castle was to be confiscated in the name of the King of Rompavia, the guards at the gate surrendered without protest. Beric was in the capital, and such a charge in the name of King Alexander was not to be ignored. Without their master, they were leaderless and had no directive to deal with the king's army.

~ * ~

Hannibal, the eunuch-slave, sat close to Sarah's cell. He had been holding her hand through the bars where she had pulled the straw mattress and arranged her blankets. The one day that her sister was to be parted from her had turned into an endless night. Without the sun, there was no knowing when it was day, or when it was night. And still Beric and Michela did not return.

The song, *Stepping Stones*, had grown silent, and Sarah's pale wan face worried Hannibal. He brought her fresh oranges, and when she would not eat them, he squeezed the juice into a chalice for her.

Now, leaning his head on the bars, he saw that she slept. Reaching through, he pulled the blankets around her, tucking them in, slapping away a large rat as it snuffled around her feet attempting to crawl in beside his small young charge. Shifting his large frame, Hannibal prepared to fall asleep himself. He knew it was not many hours until sunrise.

The sound of boots pounded out, moving with intent down the stone steps, descending into the very dungeon itself. Hannibal was suddenly awake, alert. He stood as flickering lights from torches chased the shadows from the entrance to this house of horrors.

Two dungeon keepers woke and clambered to their feet. Could it be possible that the master had returned and had come below at such an hour?

The captain of the king's army entered the dungeon, followed by many men-at-arms, all brandishing weapons.

"Where is the child? Is there a little girl locked down here?" The captain's voice projected his disbelief. This chamber was obviously used for punishing and torturing the subjects of Beric's displeasure. Both dungeon-keepers, facing extended bayonets, pointed to the end of the chamber.

Striding to the end of the dungeon, the captain stood in front of Hannibal.

"I'm looking for Miss Sarah Raynor," he said. "I have orders, from the king, to rescue her from Lord Beric's dungeon and take her to Avingworth. Where is she?"

"You will not... harm her?" Hannibal asked, knowing that he had no rights to challenge this captain, but was prepared to protect Sarah with his life if necessary.

"We're not here to harm Miss Sarah, but to rescue her. We wish to take her to her sister, Lady Michela."

"She's sleeping. It be best if she sleeps... she has not slept well down here..."

"No, neither would I," the captain said grimly. He moved closer to the bars, staring at the small girl sleeping just on the other side. His eyes circled the contents of the small cell: six candles, all lit, the food, the books, a rug hung in a place that would obscure the child's view of the larger chamber. In a moment, the captain knew that Hannibal had been Sarah's lifeline, her sanity. And as he stared again at Sarah, the captain recognized the child as the same one he had seen on the side of the road, crying. His mind flew to his own little daughter, the same size, with the same golden hair. He wished he had reported the two he had seen on the road—perhaps *this* bizarre scene would have been avoided.

"Bring the keys and unlock the door!" he called. Then to Hannibal, he said, "Carry the child up to a carriage and stay with her. I'll have some food and blankets brought. We'll leave for the capital right away. The king's orders must be obeyed."

The captain of the king's army congratulated himself. He could fulfill King Alexander's command and return with the dear little girl. All the way, from the capital to Clifton, the captain had hoped he was not being sent on the proverbial wild goose chase. It seemed like a fairy tale, rescuing a captive maiden in distress, saving her from her incarceration in a dark dungeon.

The captain and the army had yet to return to the capital and hear of Beric's performance with the pistols. They had left Avingworth before Michela had gone for the test. On the word of Janice and Laurissa, King Alexander had sent his army to carry out his orders regarding Beric's castle and its youngest prisoner.

Sarah stirred in Hannibal's arms; realizing who was carrying her, she closed her eyes and continued sleeping. Not until the sun lifted its radiant eye to chase away the night did Sarah wake to discover she was in a carriage, traveling to the capital to be with her beloved sister.

Feeling so happy and excited that she was almost sick, Sarah ate the fruit Hannibal gave her and as the countryside passed her vision, she began to hum. No longer did the song feel stale. The dark murkiness of the dungeon had vanished and a new day had been born.

~ * ~

Michela awoke at dawn, and the two doctors watching over her were stunned to see her conscious. The second doctor had agreed with the first. After a long consultation together out of Michela's bedchamber, both had told the king they did not expect Michela to gain consciousness again. Then, an hour before sunrise, she was pronounced to be in a coma. Lady Michela would die in the next twenty-four hours, it was announced.

The king still sat beside Michela, but she did not recognize him. It seemed to her that her father had been with her all night and she had held his hand.

"Please... I'm very thirsty," she said.

King Alexander moved away, and one of the doctors took his place. The middle-aged physician helped her to sit and took a tumbler of cool water from the other doctor's outstretched hand. She drank it all and asked for food. The doctor told her that it was not wise for her to eat.

Frowning, Michela lay back on the pillows, her eyes upon the doctor's face. "Who are you?" she asked, suddenly remembering, in a torrent of clear images, all that had happened in the last week. This man could not be her father. "Father is dead," she said aloud.

"I'm a doctor," he answered simply.

Closing her eyes, Michela thought of the events of last night. She saw Beric, with the pistols, throwing them at her face—the glint from the blade of his dagger. She remembered the king, his eyes upon hers. Then she blinked as she recalled how everything had vanished from her eyes and from her comprehension. Something had hit her head.

"Is... is King Alexander... safe?" she asked.

"Yes. King Alexander was not hurt at all," the doctor said, looking across at the other. They could not believe her clear speech and were amazed she could remember what had happened, where she was, that her father was dead. But such lucidity was common before death came, their eyes told each other.

"I feel hungry," she said, and asked, "May I eat something, please?"

"It's best for you to rest, Lady Michela," one doctor said. As if he needed to say something that pertained to normal life, he added, "When you've slept some more, we'll see if you are able to tolerate some food."

He waited for her eyes to close then turned to meet the solemn gaze of the king.

"She's very ill," the doctor whispered. The king bowed his head. Had he not sat by her side and prayed all night that God would spare her? Was God not stronger and mightier than any doctor... or king? It was God who could save and heal; they must pray; all they could do was pray.

When Michela next woke, the room was still dim. Light had been prevented from entering the bedchamber by securing the heavy triple-lined window drapes closed.

A form was slumped in a chair beside the bed. It was the king, snatching a few minutes sleep. Due to the long sleepless night, he was now very tired. As he was not wearing his crown, Michela did not recognize him at first, but knew he had been with her all night. It had not been her father who had held her hand, but this man.

Then it dawned on her that this was King Alexander. He slept, and his face relaxed like that of a young boy's. The frown had smoothed itself and there was no trace of cynicism on his handsome face. She watched him, thinking about the King's Test—the dwarf, the straw, the gold—wishing she could question him about it all. *Nothing is as it seemed,* she told herself. *I jumped to all the wrong conclusions.*

She blinked and then focused on the serious faces of two ladies, Laurissa and Janice.

Then the king woke, blinking and trying, unsuccessfully, to prevent a yawn.

Pulling herself into a sitting position, Michela turned the blanket back. She spoke to the women. "My dress is crumpled. How long have I been here?" She wondered if it were only a short time. "I feel as if I've slept a whole day away."

Both ladies rushed to her side, and the king sat up straight. Michela felt embarrassed because she was on a bed wearing a crumpled dress with her hair in such disarray.

"It's all right, dear," Laurissa said, "You've a nasty bang on your head and the doctors said that you must not be disturbed... he... they... they thought you would sleep... all day." How could they tell Michela about the announcement made, that she would not regain consciousness... that she was not expected to live?

"I must rise... Beric... has he gone back to Clifton?"

"Beric will not threaten or harm you... ever again," King Alexander said. Sensing her embarrassment because of his presence there, he felt at a loss to explain. "You must rest, Lady Michela. We have been very concerned... for you."

"I feel much better," she said, but lay back on the pillows arranged behind her by Laurissa. Janice drew the rugs up over her dress again and went in search of the doctors.

Afraid to take her hand, lest he upset her, the king nevertheless drew his chair closer to the bed. "You were very brave last night, Michela. You saved my life."

Their eyes met, and Michela did not look away. His eyes were filled with love, kindness, and concern, but somewhere in their depths, Michela recognized pain.

"I took the bullets out of the pistols," Michela explained. "It was in the sitting room of the apartment. Beric left his jacket on the couch. How could I resist?" She smiled, still feeling a dull throb in the side of her head, but also feeling much better. "I put the bullets under a floor rug in my room... do you think they might explode if someone treads on them?" She reached her trembling fingers to feel the lump on her temple.

"My goodness... it's big," she said, turning to look into the king's astonished face. "Did you manage to arrest Beric? He would not be easy to take. Silly man, pointing a pistol at the king... but I'm sure you've put him somewhere safe?"

"Yes," he replied, finding it difficult to comprehend; she was holding an intelligent conversation and remembering last night. It was only last night! The doctors had whispered that even if, by an amazing miracle, she survived, she would be unconscious for a long time and possibly brain-damaged because the back of her head had been injured when she had fallen to the floor. Had they not just announced that she was comatose and would not regain consciousness?

King Alexander broke the awkward silence, asking a question that perplexed him. "Why... why did you stand in front of me when Beric pointed the pistol at me? You knew he could not shoot me if you had removed the bullets."

"I... I wasn't sure..." Michela replied, trying to think why she had sidestepped. She blushed, knowing it had been a spontaneous movement; she had wanted to be sure Beric could not shoot the king.

"Father... he... said that a firearm should always be treated as if it were loaded, even if one felt sure it wasn't..."

"You protected me," he said, and his voice was very deep. "You deliberately protected me, Michela." Reaching out very slowly, he gently lifted her small hand into the warmth of his own.

"You're very brave, and I love you very much," the king said.

Michela blushed a deeper shade. She sighed and relaxed her hand, feeling the strength of his. She believed his words were because she had stood between him and Beric. Even now, Michela could not fathom why she had done that. She knew she did not want him to die, but she was sure that she did not love him, did she? No. How could she love a man, a king, who wanted a wife who spun straw into gold? Closing her eyes, she suddenly thought of Sarah. Her hand and body tensed.

"What is it?"

"Sarah. What will happen to Sarah?" Michela asked.

"She is, I believe, on the way here, to be with you." He hoped this was true, but no word had been received. He wished he had ordered fore riders to bring him news of the takeover of Beric's castle.

"She's coming here?" Michela's face brightened. Relaxing back on the pillows, she closed her eyes. The doctors had been in the room for some time now, having come with Laurissa, listening to this tender conversation, feeling sure that Michela's end was near.

"You've been with me... a long time," Michela said. "Thank you for taking care of Sarah..."

Looking up at the doctor's serious faces, King Alexander wondered what they based their prognosis on. The size of the bruise was certainly ominous; it had blackened both Michela's eyes. But now it seemed to have stopped swelling and she rested peacefully. Surely she would recover? He leaned over Michela and kissed her forehead. She did not move. He gently kissed her lips, finding them warm and soft. She sighed and a faint smile tinged her lips.

One doctor rushed to her side, feeling the pulse at her neck. He raised his eyebrows, obviously surprised that her pulse was strong and she still lived.

Standing to his full height, the king looked down at his newfound love. He had heard all that had been said in that chamber with Beric. His most challenging task, if Michela recovered, would be to explain why he had allowed Chezney and Tippet to design such a test. The test had helped him find Michela, but would she ever understand why such a test had been necessary?

The doctor stepped close to his side, whispering in the king's ear, "It will not be long now, Your Majesty; we believe her time is very short."

King Alexander frowned at him, then looked at the other doctor. He wondered about these doctors, and realized that they were strangers to him. Why did they persist in their conclusion that Michela would die?

Tippet and Chezney entered the guest chamber, bringing papers and announcing important appointments that either had to be attended to or would have to be further postponed, or cancelled.

But King Alexander could think of nothing but that his first and only love had been prognosticated to be dying. Why did he not believe it? How could he leave her here to die alone? How could he even consider matters of state?

<h1 style="text-align:center">Fourteen</h1>

"Michela, Michela... oh, please wake up. Don't die..." Sarah's sweet soft voice came to Michela's ears.

Opening her eyes, Michela held her arms out to Sarah. King Alexander had kept his word. Sarah was here.

The little girl sobbed, heartbroken. Michela stroked her sister's hair.

"It's all right, darling, it's all right. I've just been sleeping. I didn't think I'd sleep again, but I have. And I feel much better now."

Sarah ceased weeping. She looked at her sister's face. "Oh, Michela, it's a dreadful bruise... but please don't die. Don't die."

"No, darling, not today," Michela said, smiling widely. She looked down at the mauve dress, all crumpled. "Perhaps then, if I'm not going to heaven today, I should have a fresh dress to wear." Looking up, Michela's eyes met with the king's serious stare. She blushed, having not realized he was there.

"Thank you so much for bringing Sarah to me. I've been lying on this bed far too long. I wish to wash and change into something fresh. And, please excuse me for saying so again, but I'm very hungry and would like to eat something. I'm feeling so much better! Perhaps, Your Majesty, if Beric is no longer to be our guardian, we could discuss our future?"

"Beric is in the king's prison," Sarah said as if imparting something new to her sister. Tears slid down Sarah's face. She had been told that Michela was not expected to live many more hours. She clung to Michela and sobbed loudly.

Michela stared around at all the serious faces and felt she was the centerpiece in a funeral procession. "I'd really like to rise, and walk with Sarah in the fresh air, please," she said.

The king swallowed. The doctors had again verbalized their prognosis, and he, the king, had decided to stay with Michela until her end came. But here she was, sitting up and asking to rise! How was he to answer her?

Leaning toward the king's ear, the doctor said softly, "Grant her request, Sire; there's nothing to be lost."

~ * ~

The sun was sinking in a blazing summer sky when Michela, Sarah, the king, with many attendants following in melancholy, walked in the palace gardens. Fountains lifted fingers of sparkling water that glittered reflections of crimson. Surprised to be feeling so weak on her legs, Michela leaned on the king's arm and allowed him to direct her to sit on a garden seat.

Hannibal—dressed, not as a slave, but as a privileged royal attendant—took Sarah by the hand, and, followed by a small retinue, they walked away in the opposite direction. Sarah did not protest, but complied sadly. While her sister had partaken of her meal, Sarah had been told that the king wished to have time alone with Michela.

~ * ~

"I've been thinking about your test, Your Majesty. I feel sure that you had someone different in mind from a wife who could spin straw into gold for you," Michela said.

"I should not tire you by speaking of it, Michela. It's of no account... now..." the king said sadly.

"It is... to me," Michela said softly. "Please explain why you designed the test... I feel that I came to conclusions about it that were far from the truth..."

Remembering Michela's denunciation of John the dwarf, King Alexander knew that she had believed him to be a king who wanted a wife who could spin straw into gold. And it was because of his test that this funereal cloud hung over her now.

"If you could look at the kingdom of Rompavia as a whole," he began, looking at her face to gain confidence that she followed his words, "and if you put aside yourself and perhaps even myself, you will see that the kingdom is steeped in superstitious beliefs and is a fertile bed for evil occult practices. The majority of its people depend on omens and incantations for each and every one of their daily decisions..."

"Yes, I've seen that, Your Majesty," Michela agreed, giving the king assurance to continue.

"Please call me Alexander, Michela," he said before continuing. "In the first four years of my reign, Michela, I tried to make changes, and was somewhat successful in this city, Avingworth. Then when my mother died, I was lonely and we... my counselors and I, believed that a good wife would be of benefit... to me... for the future of Rompavia and the security of the throne.

"I did not want a wife who had to consult the stars—who would declare herself unable to eat, or travel on certain days because of cards and palmistry, etcetera..."

"No, Alexander."

"No." The king paused to look down into Michela's eyes. It was as though time stood still.

The bruise across her brow was disconcerting, but other than looking very pale, Michela appeared very much alive and obviously able to follow everything he said. There were no signs of drowsiness.

"Please continue..." Michela urged.

"The choices of gifts told us the values each maiden had... and we gained an insight as to the advice she listened to, and if she had any wisdom, any prowess, any opinions of her own."

"I see..." Michela said, thinking of the jewelry and the charms.

"Then the... the charade, you called it... yes, the charade... spinning straw into gold." The king was silent for a few seconds, choosing the words he needed to explain. He did not know where to begin.

"Would you believe, Michela, that some girls declared they had spun the straw into gold, even after John came in and revealed himself? Another young maiden called John a liar... one called me... a liar... she declared she had spun the gold herself and was going to spin me some more, she said, having already given away our first child, she would have given away our second..."

"Did many take the second test?" Michela had to ask.

"Enough to make me feel sick," the king admitted truthfully. "All of them, prepared to give away an unborn child to satisfy their appetite for power. To become queen! I'm afraid I still shudder to imagine any of them as my wife, as my mentor, my queen." He turned as an attendant brought a warm cloak. Taking the garment, he placed it around Michela's shoulders. The sun had set and the summer evening had turned cooler.

"I need a wife who is wise, one who sees beyond the treasures and values of the moment, one who looks to the future for the good of others, one who is not selfishly thinking just of herself." He drew a deep breath, and said softly, "I have found her, Michela; you are the one."

Michela did not reply; she thought over the reasons he had given for the test. How hard it must have been for him to learn the extent of the superstition in the kingdom. How lonely he had been.

"Your reaction to the test was what I had hoped for, but had never seen. You behaved even more wisely than I imagined, or hoped, anyone could be. Your very anger at the charade was the reason the test was designed. At first, I thought someone had discovered our purpose behind the test; I thought you were putting on an act, and I even wondered if you were overdoing your own charade!"

Michela realized how much his thoughts and beliefs were like her own. She had never felt so secure in all her life. Just to be near him was bliss.

"I wanted a wife who spoke the truth and looked ahead, not making rash promises that she would not wish to keep, one who did not follow superstitions as so many in our kingdom do..." The king had almost exhausted himself. He grasped her hand and held it tight.

"I could never agree to give away a child!" Michela said, her eyes filling with tears. She tried to pull her hand away. Something was happening inside her, and she felt frightened by the intensity of her own emotions.

"I know you couldn't," the king said. "Neither could I." His hand tightened.

"It did make me very angry, Your Majesty; it was a horrible test," Michela said, shuddering. He moved closer to her, placing his arm around her. She did not pull away, but rested her head on his broad shoulder.

Michela's thoughts suddenly felt torn, and her head ached. Nothing was as it had seemed. King Alexander was earnest and kind, tenderhearted, and very genuine about finding the right wife for the good of his kingdom. He was all that she had dreamed a good husband could be... but he was King of Rompavia!

She felt tired and tearful, and she closed her eyes.

Footmen lighted lamps in the garden, and still the king and the lady sat on the seat beside the fountain. His arm around her, and her head on his shoulder, neither spoke. The king could not believe that she would die soon. As if this thought transferred itself to her, she stiffened and drew away.

"What is it?" he asked.

"Why... is everyone... so concerned? Why is Sarah... so sure I'm going to die?"

"The doctors were... are... very concerned, Michela... they believed you would not regain consciousness..."

"I... I was just sleeping," Michela said. "How long did the doctors say that I would live?"

"It is of no consequence now, Michela. You are obviously... obviously..." He could not continue.

"Yes, I am... obviously... very much alive. And I want to know, please. How long did they say?"

"Two days," he admitted, and could not prevent tears filling his eyes. Turning his head downward, he blinked them away.

"Alfena!" Michela accused. "Your doctors consult with Alfena." She laughed, "I'm not going to die, Alexander. I'm going to live. But I won't be happy for you if Alfena and those two doctors and any other followers have a den in your palace."

"Alfena?" he asked, feeling confused.

"Elisabet, Beric's wife, consulted a... a witch called Alfena... in the palace here. Did you not hear Elisabet tell me to wear an amulet? Were you not listening in the adjacent room?"

"Yes, I do remember..."

"Elisabet told me that I would die within two days if I did not wear the amulet. She got it from Alfena. Your doctors must have consulted her, and of course, they have to believe Alfena's prophecies when she speaks of blood and doom. Bad news is always easier to believe than good news. I have just a few hours to live, Alexander, the gods of Rompavia have decreed it!"

The king stood to his feet, feeling horrified at the reproof he felt from her words, and at her cynicism.

"It's no matter to ridicule, Michela!" He himself had believed the doctors' forecast and had not questioned them. That they were believing and acting upon some evil revelation seemed all the more ominous to the king. Turning he called, "Captain! Guards!"

King Alexander issued orders, demanding that Alfena be found even if the palace had to be searched, inch by inch.

Then, to Michela, he said, "Come, let us fetch Sarah and go to the chapel. We will pray, and God will give the victory. It's his battle; we must pray He will win it."

Fifteen

Alfena was never found, but proof of her activities was discovered in a room under a tower in a less-used wing of the palace.

The two doctors admitted they had consulted with Alfena and that it was Alfena's prognosis that had been passed on to the king. When further questioned, the doctors agreed that Lady Michela's physical reactions had not matched Alfena's predictions, but even so, they had chosen to believe the witch. Such a revelation caused the king to feel he was attempting the impossible! People were too stepped in superstition to change!

"In my own palace! It shows what progress we have made. None! To think of physicians depending upon superstitious prophecies above their intelligence and professional experience, is beyond me."

"It just proves that you do need a wise wife to help you in your battle, Sire," Chezney said with a twinkle in his eye.

"Yes, but I'm afraid she won't want me," the king said sadly.

"There's only one way to find out," Chezney said, "and that's to ask her. Besides, the forty-eight hours are almost up, and Lady Michela is improving all the time, is she not?"

"Yes... but I've ordered guards to stay at the door to her chamber; I fear someone will try to make Alfena's prophecy come true," the king said. "Who knows our enemies, even in our palace? Our own doctors encouraged such as Alfena to conduct her moonlighting here."

"You're wise, Sire. The doctors still maintain that Alfena declared there would be death before the forty-eight hours are up."

~ * ~

Michela slept well that night, having requested that Sarah be allowed to sleep with her in the large four-poster bed in the first guest chamber. She woke to a clear bright day, telling the ladies in her bedchamber that her headache had vanished.

When Sarah awoke, Michela said, "Life is wonderful, Sarah, isn't it? We're together, and we don't have to worry about Beric or Elisabet. Or Percival." She smiled, feeling deliciously relaxed and at ease.

Laurissa entered the chamber, and Michela asked, "Do you think we may stay here for a few days?"

"We were hoping you would ask that," Laurissa said. "You may stay as long as you like, Michela. King Alexander wants you to recover completely from your ordeals."

"Beric was our worst ordeal," Sarah said, "But he's in prison, isn't he?"

"Beric cannot harm anyone, or threaten anyone, ever again," Laurissa said, "Beric is dead. They found him dead in his cell, early last evening. An amulet he wore about his neck seeped poison... it's thought that is the cause of his death."

~ * ~

Three days later, the king invited Michela to walk with him in the garden. He thought how pale she still looked, but realized that the black dress she chose to wear added to her delicate appearance. Black was definitely not a suitable color for her, he decided. The bruise on her temple and forehead had diminished greatly, even fading in some places into obscurity.

Moving her arm from his, to hold her hand, he turned her to face him. Attendants and guards in the background knew that this was the moment. It was as if the palace itself held its breath.

Wanting only to propose, the king asked, "How are you feeling now?" It came out wrong. He did not feel nervous; he felt terrified! She was going to refuse him, he told himself. *I do not deserve her... she is far more glorious than I could have ever hoped...*

"Very well, thank you, Your Majesty."

He swallowed, and said, "I requested that you call me Alexander."

"You told me that when you believed I was going to die," she said. "Do you still want me to call you Alexander?"

"Yes. Will you forgive me?" he asked.

"Forgive you?"

"For causing you to believe I wanted a wife who could spin straw into gold... and for not checking out those superstitious doctors... and..."

Michela laughed and the king drew a deep breath. He had never seen her laugh like this and she looked incredibly beautiful, even in her black dress. He felt his heart pounding in a strange manner and he longed to kiss her.

"I have forgiven you, Alexander. I understand it all; please believe me, I don't blame you for anything, dear Alexander."

The king had never heard anyone say his name like that before.

"You've forgiven me?"

"Yes, Alexander. There really was nothing to forgive. These three days, I've been thinking... particularly about the King's Test. I realize that without the test, I'd never have come to Avingworth. I may never have known you, Alexander. I want... only... to please you, and serve you as my king... Alexander."

He did not speak.

"Also, Alexander... we must forgive Beric. Without him, I realize, we may never have met. I'm quite sure that everything bad that has happened has been a step toward... toward..."

"Michela," he interrupted, "will you marry me?"

"Yes, Alexander."

He could hardly believe his ears, and then as he looked into her eyes, he saw only love and admiration. He kissed her and it seemed all time stood still. The garden, a kaleidoscope of colors, gleamed beneath a sun that seemed to shine brighter than ever before.

All around the garden, people nudged each other and passed on the good news. The king was kissing Lady Michela... perhaps she'd said 'yes.'

"When?" he asked.

"When the time of mourning for my father is over, Alexander... if that is not too soon for you."

"Tomorrow would not be too soon, Michela. But a month will not be too long, either; I've waited six long years to meet you. I love you so much, darling. I believed I would find you, but never imagined you could be so splendid, so beautiful, so wise, so real."

"I love you, Alexander. I love you more than I could imagine I could ever love anyone..."

Then he kissed her again; and she returned his kiss. The fusion was there again, as if they belonged, forever.

~ * ~

One month later, the bells of Avingworth rang louder and longer than ever before.

King Alexander married the only maiden in the kingdom who had passed the King's Test.

And all the way down the aisle, walking behind the beautiful bride, a lovely young flower girl—the bride's beloved sister, Sarah—hummed the tune of a song in which she believed with all her young sweet heart

.

Meet Carolyn Ann Aish

Carolyn Ann Aish was born Carolyn Ann Gundesen in the small town of Waitara, Taranaki, New Zealand in 1948. She was raised in New Plymouth and now resides in Inglewood beneath the spectacular Taranaki Mountain along with her husband, Pastor Walter Aish.

The first published books in the series, "The Frencolian Chronicles," TREASURES, CASTLES, and KINGDOMS, enjoy rave reviews, creating an on-going following for Carolyn's work.

Carolyn earned a spot in the 1996 Guinness Book of Records (music section, page 144) for the longest hymn published. [2003 Guinness World Records Book also records this on page 191]. The previous record was made 800 years ago.

Among the many series Carolyn has written is "The Nine Lives of Rastus," based on the lives of Max Corkill and his beloved cat, Rastus.

Works From the Pen of Carolyn Ann Aish

Stepping Stones - Forced to leave her sister in a dungeon, Michela goes with her guardian's to take part in the 'King's Test.' Does the king really believe she can spin straw into gold?

Michela denounces the 'King's Test' as a charade. Will she find death, or will she find love?

Kind Heart - King Cyranius is a woman-hater, and Lady Jennava hates most men. This does not prevent them from secretly falling in love. But a phantom-like masked man towering between them crushes loves petals before they bloom...

Royalty, romance, mystery, escapism—this book has it all. Just remember to breathe.

Letter to Our Readers

Enjoy this book?

You can make a difference.

As an independent publisher, Wings ePress, Inc. does not have the financial clout of the large New York publishers. We can't afford large magazine spreads or subway posters to tell people about our quality books.

But we do have something much more effective and powerful than ads. We have a large base of loyal readers.

Honest reviews help bring the attention of new readers to our books.

If you enjoyed this book, we would appreciate it if you would spend a few minutes posting a review on the site where you purchased this book or on the Wings ePress, Inc. webpages at:

https://wingsepress.com

Thank You

VISIT OUR WEBSITE

FOR THE FULL INVENTORY
OF QUALITY BOOKS:

http://www.wingsepress.com

Quality trade paperbacks and downloads
in multiple formats,
in genres ranging from light romantic comedy
to general fiction and horror.
Wings has something
for every reader's taste.
Visit the website, then bookmark it.
We add new titles each month!